A Southern Tragedy, in Crimson and Yellow

For *A Southern Tragedy, in Crimson and Yellow,* Naumoff creates an extended metaphor like a poet. The novel has the grace and wonder and finality of a postmortem, where each detail is revealed, turned around and looked at from behind, from underneath.

It's about a bunch of people mostly screwing up right and left, and the remnants of a beautiful, bright heritage, and the diary of a woman driven mad by grief. By the end of the novel, there is nothing less than the whole shebang, the whole mystery of life and death and honor.

With meticulous physical descriptions, Naumoff has written not just an historical novel, or a political one, or one of personal lives and tragedies, but all those things at once.

—*Haven Kimmel*

Praise for Lawrence Naumoff's Other Books

The Night of the Weeping Women

"(Naumoff) looks at marriage honestly. What he sees is outrageously—hilariously, tragically—undeniable; and he sets it all down with effortless-looking brilliance.

—Reynolds Price

Rootie Kazootie

"A brilliant comedy of errant romance.... Plaintive, madcap, utterly seductive, Naumoff writes about marriage and faithlessness as if he were concocting an eighth Deadly Sin."

—The *Washington Post*

Taller Women

"*Taller Women* is compellingly radiant meta-fiction about male-female relationships. A scathing indictment of the way things were 'back then', i.e., now. A warning written in dazzling prose variously reminiscent of Pinter, Beckett, Robert Coover and Nathanael West."

—*Publishers Weekly*

Silk Hope, NC

"The book is funny, sad and wise in all the right places."

—*The News and Observer*

A Plan for Women

"A provocative novel . . . When Naumoff exercises his exacting sympathy, understanding and humor on the desperate moments of daily life, he brings such compassion to his characters that their struggles are heroically transformed."

—*The New York Times Book Review*

LAWRENCE NAUMOFF

A Southern Tragedy, in Crimson and Yellow

ZUCKERMAN CANNON PUBLISHERS

Zuckerman Cannon Publishers
Distributed by John F. Blair, Publisher
Winston-Salem, NC 27103
Orders: 1-800-222-9796
www.blairpub.com

LIBARY OF CONGRESS-CATALOGING-IN-PUBLICATION DATA
ISBN 0-9664316-2-6

10 9 8 7 6 5 4 3 2 1
Printed in the United States of America

To the people of Hamlet, the workers in the plant, and people everywhere living through oppressive, unjust or dangerous conditions.

To Marianne and Michael

Near Dover Foxcroft, Maine, 1970s

Lawrence Naumoff won a National Endowment for the Arts Discovery Award after finishing school at UNC in Chapel Hill. He used that money and moved to Mexico briefly, thinking he might live the expatriate writer's life, having read too many B. Traven novels. After that, he moved to Maine, farmed, ran out of money and then returned to Chatham County, near Chapel Hill, where he continues to live.

To the people of Hamlet:

This novel follows the women in a family from 1919 to 1991, the year of the fire. It follows those women from the merchant class to working chickens. The characters are not based on any family from your town.

And people of Hamlet, understand also that the workers in the chicken plant in this novel are not literally the people who worked there or died in the fire. If you spend your time trying to figure out who this or that character is, or if an event happened as it appears in this novel, you'll go nuts, because some things will seem real and actual, and other things will be made up. That's what the demands of creating a drama and a narrative do, and it's that freedom and that range of creation that makes a novel what it is—not journalism.

To all readers:

Because my other novels have, as their main character, a woman, it was likely this one would, as well. I found my character in Ellie McCorkle.

Following the women in Ellie's family opened up the history of the town of Hamlet, an amazing little place in real life that was the home of both John Coltrane and Tom Wicker.

In writing this book, I also knew I had to show why it was that people worked in a chicken plant in the first place. That seemed an easy question to answer. It wasn't. It took this entire novel to answer that.

PART I

Railroads, Hamlet and the Invention of Ice Cream

The town of Hamlet was near the towns of McColl, Cheraw and Wagram, in the part of the state known as the Sandhills, just above the South Carolina line. The Pee Dee River (imagine Lumbee Indians in canoes, and eels and catfish in the tannin-stained water) flowed west of the town, behind the hospital and past the former home for unwed mothers, past the abandoned distillery, and past the abandoned ice cream truck where an old man once lived, a hermit called Buttercup. Wild plums, blackberries and pokeweed grew along the banks of the river, and multiflora roses tangled beside the tracks of the Seaboard Air Line Railroad.

The river continued, away from Hamlet, through South Carolina and to the ocean, where it joined the Waccamaw just below Pawley's Island.

In the town itself, though, grounded and unflowing, there was a poultry processing plant, and it was because of that poultry plant that on a humid September day in 1991, people were bunched together in the streets the way that in old films entire populations congregated to watch the Martians land. The people watched the chicken plant burn. Smoke as streaked and creamy as melted

Dreamsicles squeezed out from the eaves of the flat-roofed building like crimson genies from an old Disney cartoon.

The population, which might have seen flying saucers and then skinless, red aliens walking toward them, saw, instead, human forms as soot black as dark chocolate. At the same time, they heard nothing from anyone inside. As quiet as the crowd was, as quiet as air and as breath, they heard nothing.

Buildings had burned before. Rosin-rich pine lumber burned scarlet and yellow and orange, and in the nighttime skies, before streetlights and electricity and automobiles, the flames of those old buildings were clear and lovely and terrifying for 20 miles. People did not burn that beautifully.

The town once had an opera house. Caruso sang there. That building became the movie theater just after the second world war. Children who later grew up to work and die in the fire at the chicken plant spent all day in that theater, years before they had to figure out a way to earn a living.

The fact that before television, opera had been a popular musical medium enjoyed by rich and poor was surprising to the generations brought up on television and fast food.

"Opera? You mean Oprah?"

Quick cuisine was now the main product of the local poultry enterprise. Capital Foods supplied not cultural delights of the past such as drama and music, but chicken delights, boxed presentations of legs, thighs, breasts and wings that neither sang or danced or nurtured or inspired, except on the chemical and commercial stage. Food had replaced the opera as pastime.

Want to go hear Puccini? It's in town I'm told.

Naw. Let's go to KFC.

Or better yet—How about the new Aaron Copeland special

at Burger King, the Appalachian Burger with Spring Fries and Simple Gifts child's meal.

Unemployment was just under 11% in the county in 1991. It was the chicken plant, or nothing.

Many people loved the small-town life. Some didn't, however, and left. Hamlet was the hometown of John Coltrane. Tom Wicker, born the same year as Coltrane, 1926, was from Hamlet.

In early September of 1991, at the time of the tragedy that would distinguish Hamlet forever in a new way, Bill Clinton was running for President. George Bush the father, would, in a little more than two months, carry Richmond County but lose nationwide.

The chicken plant building where Ellie McCorkle showed up the day of the fire was mostly brick. It had a concrete floor. It was 37,000 square feet, almost an acre. Seen from above, without the roof on it, the way an architect's model might have been viewed with the top lifted off, the building contained rooms for processing, marinating, cutting, mixing, trimming, and cooling, two freezer rooms and more. Lots of rooms.

It was a dangerous and illogical maze with partitions added over the years as needed and doors that led nowhere, a fire trap that no one thought could burn. How could brick and block and concrete burn?

Old mills were built on large dimension wood joists with three-inch-thick floor boards. It was the lumber from these old mills that made the expensive re-sawn flooring for custom houses today. Standing and working on a wood floor felt different than working all day on concrete. Concrete crushed your bones, went right through your shoes, up into your heels, up your spine, into your brain, and made the day headache long.

The building that became Capital Food Products was founded on cement, lime, rock and sand. The concrete for that floor would have been mixed on site in 1921, and then spread wheelbarrow by wheelbarrow and floated and troweled and finished by hand.

6,000 cubic yards of concrete were poured eight inches deep. Old wheelbarrows held an eighth of a yard and weighed 300 pounds loaded to the top. They had steel wheels. In a true act of hard labor, they were pushed and dumped 48,000 times before the floor was complete.

Concrete could be poured in the rain. It would dry anyway. It gave off heat when curing. On hot days, sweat dripped off foreheads and arms and mixed with the water evaporating across the top and made a speckled, freckly looking surface. The concrete dried white, or gray-white, depending on the mix, and took a couple of weeks to reach strength.

Concrete lasted centuries, longer than people and longer than the buildings above it. It would not burn. It remained. The Romans invented concrete. Thus the Ruins.

The building had been a Buttercup Ice Cream plant before it processed chicken parts. In the South, concrete pouring and finishing, masonry and tile work had traditionally been done by black men. Carpentry and electrical and plumbing mostly by white, but bricks and mortar and tile, black.

The men gathered together, however, and did their jobs and built the structure. People from all stations in life joined up to provide other people with places to work, where more people came together and made ice cream cups or skinned chickens or whatever was asked of them. Within the buildings there formed a congregation of sorts, all temporarily believing in what they were doing.

They talked to each other while together, creating the simple language of work not based on the eloquent delivery of theory and analysis, but based on the common language of shared faith, despair and hardship.

All that mixing and pouring and finishing work, then, done 70 years earlier, remained, and provided the foundation and boundaries of all the work yet to come, defined, then, the sense and reach of the job, hard, unyielding, stained with product and human effort, poured into place in the town, and therefore into the lives of thousands of people, an act originally of monumental human toil just to pour the concrete on the ground, to cover the earth in that one spot that then limited and ordained that one place on the planet where people would gather and do what was asked of them.

With all that heart and soul and belief, they gathered together and became, for a little while, the same. That was the nature of work.

They were doing the best they could at that moment in their lives, choosing to make a statement they themselves did not understand by working there in the world of processed chickens, but mostly just surviving to the next day and working, simply working, like all the people who'd been on that slab before them, working and surviving and trusting that some good would come of it.

They showed up for work each day and they had faith. The gift of faith worked best by keeping it unopened, talking about it, and manufacturing belief, which is what the work at this chicken plant actually did in its most sublime few moments each day.

It processed not simply parts of the two-legged winged beasts, but people, a place where they came together as they had in the ice cream days and before that in the construction of the edifice, not an ark of worship, but of work, which was, for people who made for themselves pieces of hope out of pieces of bird, a similar collective experience.

Ice cream and chickens.

Black and white skin.

Owners and workers.

Hot and cold.

Lips and beaks.

Blood and milk.

Flesh and bone.

And breasts. Lots of breasts. The mythic remnant of nurture and desire and safety, the iconic shape and texture, the bosom of feathery motherhood now simply paddled along in rivers of heated grease, the breaded, eviscerated gland of feminine identity, torn loose from the birds' bodies by women workers, cooked by them, packed, frozen, boxed, shipped and then consumed. Whether the chicken or the egg came first was moot when it came to meat. The breast was queen for the kings, the legs, the thighs, the wings, princes in the royal ritual of feed.

CHAPTER 2

_____

On the day of the fire, Ellie McCorkle would read an ancestral diary, and it, like the fire, would change her life.

A little more than 70 years before the fire, in 1919, Emily Austin's eight-year-old daughter died. A cemetery had recently been established and the daughter would be the first person buried there. Her dog, Tips, followed the hearse. There were no people between the dog and the coffin. The dog walked at the head of the procession, and the family followed. No one arranged this. It was simply that Tips didn't want to let her mistress out of her sight. She knew Caroline was in that coffin. She had remained by the bed as the girl faded away, and watched her placed into the sad little box.

(from Emily's diary—on the train returning home weeks after the funeral.)

I am in the berth of the Pullman car. Shadows and shapes and restless, flitting wisps of what seem to be hair appear on the ceiling, single, loose strands. I reach up to collect them and make them neat around my missing daughter's face, to comb them with my fingers and stroke them into place. Everywhere I go I see Caroline, shoes that look like hers, a strange girl's hand and I want to hold it, I almost do, I nearly take her hand in mine and I might. I will then be arrested or put away somewhere. I even named her after the state. I was in love with being alive then. Now, forever more, I will think of her whenever I see or hear it called. The North of Caroline and the South of Caroline, all around me.

Weeds and stunted trees as poor and bent as failing Japanese bonsai surrounded the newly cleared burial site. After the coffin was lowered into the ground, the dog remained while everyone else left. Dry axled wagon wheels squeaked as the hubs scraped on each somber revolution. Reins tapped the wide backs of draft horses while dust kicked up low to the ground and settled back, no wind to carry it further.

(diary): I can't sleep and I won't. At first, people told me that I would get used to her being away. I believed it. I have always believed what people said if it meant that something good would happen, because it usually did.

Moisture, maybe it's dew, maybe it's early morning, drips down the window and I could say it's like tears but it's not because it's cool and will stop when the sun rises. I will never stop until empty. My own tears are hot and leave streaks down my face and people tell me to wash up, to clean up, I'll feel better, but I don't wipe them away. I look at myself and see my face streaked and puffy like a punished, heart-broken child's, and I want it that way.

The cemetery, like most of the land in the Sandhills in the early 20th century, had little shade. Trees grew slowly in the poor soil. The ground cover was thin and low and similar to what naturally grew on the coast, and the burial grounds looked much like the scrabbly graveyards seen in movies of the old West, like Boot Hills in a hundred towns, except Caroline's family put up a white column in classical lines that pointed, as it narrowed, to the heavens, as if sighting the ascent of their daughter's soul.

(diary): This numb, private room in the Pullman is like a tomb. There is no air. It's heavy like anesthetic—ethery and full of demons. My own curtains are not tightly pulled as my husband's. He said, I won't bother you until you tell me it's all right. He would never look at me with that strange desirous need if I told him what it looked like. I will put him in a book. If I wrote a book, I would. If I was allowed. It's not proper, but a diary is all right.

(diary): There is my other daughter, Milly. I remember, somebody said it in a letter, that my days will now be as bare and scrubbed of sensuality as the whitewashed walls of a hospital room and I thought when I read the comparison that it was wrong, because it would have been better to say the whitewashed walls of a cell in a dry climate where even the blood of living people dries up inside them, like powder or sand under their skin, in their heart. Death in a dry, hot climate is cleaner than what occurs with subtropically lushful death for the gilded classes of the Carolinas. I'd rather die in a soapsuds box lined with old carpet, like a cat behind the stove.

Emily's husband was a builder and merchant in early Hamlet, and in the boom period that the end of the nineteenth century and the beginning of the twentieth brought with it, he sold his houses as fast as he could build them, bought commercial property on Main Street, built the buildings and rented them, and bought, as well, farmland. He invested in the Pintsch Gas Works, which made gas from burning coal. That type of gas was used in locomotive headlights.

(diary): When I married Mr. Austin, I thought of him as a dense medium for my weakness. I thought of myself as weak. I am certainly now a sunken, expressionless form of resentment and pity, thin lips and a skeleton face. I am a contraction of confusion and legs and belly. I am dry and breastless, a furtive eye looking inward. I am prodigal with no redemption. I am my dead daughter and if I am not I want to be. The minister has nothing to say that could be true. I decide that belief is a mean, gushing condition like hysteria.

(diary): She was the freckled child. She was my grandmother's favorite and my grandmother was my best friend. She told me Caroline had the unanxious face that she had been waiting to see. She was long dead before Caroline's lungs changed that face, before suffering changed all that. Why?

I haven't seen Milly in four weeks. I will weep and it will be all right. Be grateful for the acceptance of dizzy, female hysteria. We can have that. Be that. It's understood. Allowed. Bursts out like a tipped-over railcar full of people.

One of the early hotels was constructed by the Bridges family. It wasn't far from the distillery, whose whiskey was shipped out of Hamlet by rail. It was packaged in clay jugs and glass bottles.

(diary): A lantern-jawed man with prominent eyes. I keep hearing that phrase. I see the undertaker and his long, horse-like face and the eyeballs about to roll out of his head, as if they were too big, as if he had been given eyes from someone else that didn't fit but were about to roll out. I was afraid and sorry for him. He took Caroline and I thought how lucky she can't see him. She would be more affected than me, but show it less. She was brave and I am not.

Copper-distilled, mountain whiskeys and brandies:
New Corn Whiskey, $1.25 per gallon.
Medium Old, $1.50 per gallon.
Old Corn Whiskey, $2.00 per gallon.
Apply Brandy, $2.25 per gallon.
Peach Brandy, $2.25 per gallon.
Grape Brandy, $2.25 per gallon.
Ginger Brandy, $2.00 per gallon.
Peach and Honey, $2.00 per gallon.
Half Rye and Half Corn, $1.75 per gallon.
Beer $1.00 per dozen bottles.

(diary): We are scrupulous. We are punctual. We eat our meals as if we ourselves are clocks. I wanted, not long ago, to wiggle like a sideshow freak, my hair on fire, possessed, sucking everything that hung down, tassels and braids and ferny fronds that made my tongue dance inside my mouth, which must be kept shut. I lift my arms and no one's there. I am an arduous and chronic vacancy. Caroline wanted to be everything, to see everything, and I wanted to be there with her. I ran behind my little girls and I think they laughed. I think I heard them laugh. I think I laughed.

All distillery shipments were made the day of the order. This was a source of income for the town and the money stayed in the town. Merchants who owned the means of production lived in the town and profit remained in the town.

(diary): We stop and I see a woman on the deck of the station and beside her is Milly but it's not. We're not home. The girl has a round face and braids that are too tight and no one in my house braids my girls' hair too tight because I won't allow it. German and Austrian nannies. Immigrant maids afraid of me. I never enjoyed that. I let them go. My daughters ran like boys, long strided hounds across the grass, curling up like lions in the high weeds, always together, and I stand at the window and want to be out there with them. I won't wear black anymore. How did I know I am supposed to wear it for two years? How do I know everything I know?

The first buildings downtown, like in most early commercial districts, were wood. They faced each other across the dirt street which had no sidewalks. The structures had porches and big signs announcing their services:

"Yadkin River Power Company—Electric Flat Irons—Thirty Day Free Trial"

"Fox Drug Company—Meet me at the Fountain"

Usually, every decade or so, there was a fire. Some buildings would burn and the new ones would be brick and masonry and steel, the owners and town officials hoping that the fires would be a thing of the past, from then on. In Hamlet, the main street of buildings after the turn of the century were, except for the Seaboard Hotel and the similar train station, brick and steel.

(diary): My Christian Science neighbors tell me there can be no error, there can be no wrong. They read the new books by Mrs. Eddy but her own child was taken from her so what am I to believe. What did she do that the authorities took her own child away from her? They call that thinking mental malpractice, the dwelling on what we call reality, and they say to each other, they tell me, they will not allow themselves to be mental malpracticed. They don't think you can be sick unless you admit to being sick. They don't think you can die unless you say the words. They seem to believe that only by saying the words can the illness gain power over you. They give me their sad, faulty smiles, but they never say that Caroline has died, that she's with the Lord, that she's no longer here. I wonder if they think she's still here? Can they do that? I can't.

The men speak in polished epigrams, in the demolishing syllogisms of certainty, with suffocating and antagonistic monotony. I want to hang the mantle of shame around their necks, around their waists like a corset, cinched and crimped so that nothing moves, so that they are flushed in the face from the gluttony of their own words, a septic meal of untruth.

Later.

I am a clumsy forgery now. I was so good at it. I am the forger of my own life. I may simply go mad and spin around like a child. I tremble inside like the hind quarters of an old nag. I am as dry as the skin of a dead, sun-baked opossum, my pointed snout bared in a silly grin.

The trains and their corporations survived everything back then, the wars, the epidemics, the Depression. Tracks were laid on the ground wherever they were needed. The trains began to use that ground, that piece of land. Before that, the ground was something else, a place where animals walked or people labored, where crops grew, where some things died and birth occurred like a slippery accident. Dust, wood and iron.

(diary): Once the lungs filled with air, and the air filled with blood, it was an uneasy witness to stop it. The body convulsed forward, the diaphragm clenched again and again and the eyes, open and on you, begged for help. The little hands opened wide and the arms reached for you. Just one more breath, please. Just one. You witnessed that. Whoever you were.

I am transformed. I am a bird. I am a Siamese cat. All the fashionable people have Siamese now.

My paleness makes me more beautiful. I want to be brown as a Negress, as an Indian, and barefoot, like some unproclaimed native, an opportuness in a bed of flowers, not a grave, but above the earth, a lurking blight of unecstasy, my cultivated leisure weedy and barren and my reflection painted like Wedgwood patterns, hallucinating under the bubbly tongue of that physician, inside the lantern-faced mortician, no fruity bloom pinched and daubed on my cheeks with fine bristles like the decoration I was meant to be.

I will break me on the floor, from the roof, out the window. I can smell the ether and the camphor. I will smell it forever. It is the odor of my skin and breath. Wasn't it clever to live and die in Hamlet? All the rails, both north and south, from the west as far as you could ride and from the coast, all the rail lines intersect right at the very heart of the town. Coffins that are rosary beaded and carved in walnut or with mahogany gargoyles have been laid inside the cars passing through town sealed with diphtheriate children.

Caroline dies and I am sent away because I won't recover. I won't understand. I won't admit. Caroline dies and I smile and they want to close my lips. Everything must close. Stay closed. I took the little metal puller that forces the eye onto the hook in closing shoes so tight they stop the circulation, and I stabbed my hand one day. Someone sang *O Paradise* as we walked back, as I was led away, and the indecency of grief felt so good. I wanted to be indecent forever. I guess that's why I smiled.

(diary): The men had a nip, they called it that, a nip of old, so very old and so very expensive Cognac and I continued to smile. I can't say that I was with my girl then, but it was as if she stopped off to see me and I felt she was there, not simply with me, but within me, a part of me again, and that I could be her forever, I would be like she was, except for the damnable, pursuing indecency of grief.

(diary): I am a quiet woman who was finely patterned and shaped, a crystal in a window reflecting other people, a vase for the youthful flower that I was, I made myself, they made myself, they made me into a vase into which I put myself. A nice trick. I go off the balcony, off the roof, under the train, into the opium sleep, with exotic cocained desires racking me like shivers and laughter. Profane vigils of excess are all around me.

(diary): I am an elaborate precaution of rocks and no slim ankle upon Mr. Austin's Turkish rug I think, remembering barefootedness and then the rub of the pile against my back. It is morning,

the part of morning that the good and proper and decent people call the morning. I am home. I can see the station, the turrets of the hotel, the Queen Anne of Hamlet, gilded spires onto which I can impale. I love you. You.

One of Emily's best friends, part of the book and Flinch club, married in December at 7 A.M. in the First Presbyterian Church. Emily was matron of honor. Afterwards, the couple left on the train, whose schedule had dictated the early hour of the ceremony. They took with them a box of dewberries, a blackberry relative, which were grown on the first commercial dewberry farm in the state, one of the properties in which Mr. Austin had an interest.

(diary): Thirty-five acres of pink and pale flowers. A painted world. Pastel, for awhile. Then bleeding berries. Thorny fish hook vines. Weddings. Death, slow, pale, dark, liver colored, yellow and brown.

I am home. I am in Hamlet. The hub of the east coast. We pull in to the rail yard, the train pulled in, I within it, pulled back to town.

I'm home. I'm back home. I look at her photograph and cry. I do it again and again.

The rail yard received and classified and dispatched. That was its function and its process. It processed the trains and sent them on. It was done through brilliant scientific simplicity, devised by the genius of labor, by men who studied how it could be that if they allowed something to move of its own weight, and altered it just by inches, here and there, it would continue on at walking speed, as if the men walking beside it were still beside the horse, guiding it and urging it, the cars cut loose from the engines and moving around the classification yard as if by magic, the result of the practical wisdom of work and vision.

It used the laws of gravity. It used the hump. A thousand tons of rail stock rolled by itself across the hump, over that perfectly calculated rise, directed and aimed, the momentum governed supernaturally, metaphysically, as if divinity was truly, and not just in sermons, but was truly in the labor of mankind. God and man combined perfectly in this effort, the connection of the divine and the desire of human order and efficiency.

There was always something spiritual and inspired whenever work could be made less killing, less draft like, so that a man or woman at work was less a horse or mule and more a thinking creation. Gravity, not muscle or even steam or diesel, moved the separated freewheeling cars to their perfect destination. The inventor of the gravity classification yard, that is, of the divinely inspired method of moving weight and freight and people, was something of a deity or saint in what he had given the working class. Here, in Hamlet, was the biggest self-propelled, self-rationalizing classification yard on the East Coast.

Something went wrong, though. In spite of the perfection of past effort and thought and device and invention, by the time of Capital Foods and the supersonic chicken that sped through its entire life in five weeks and ended up on a biscuit four days later, so that when someone bit into it, it almost squawked so recently it had been alive, something had gone wrong in town. The people showed up, like they were supposed to, and they went to work, and they died.

CHAPTER 3

Ellie's family continues: Great-grandma Milly.

"There's going to be a wreck," Milly yelled.

It was January 12, 1920, six months since Caroline had died. Emily had recovered from her despair. She spent a lot of time outdoors and had been seen running through the yard.

"Mom."

A special excursion train carrying 612 "Negro" passengers had left Durham on the annual trip for the families of the St. Joseph African Methodist Episcopal Sunday School. They were traveling to Charlotte.

"Two trains are going to crash," Milly said.

The train came through Hamlet. After it left, it was learned by telegraph that Number 44, a freight, was fifteen miles away, heading right for it. A mistake had been made and both trains were on the same track.

There were no wireless radios on the trains and unless someone could get in a car and race to a midpoint before the trains arrived, they would crash. If the people could get there first, a group could be sent in one direction to flag down the excursion train, while another could be running down the rails to flag down the freight.

"I heard it at the station."

She was seven years old. It was four in the afternoon. She had gone with her friends to the station to see who might be stopping off there. Once she shook hands with a Mr. Rockefeller and his wife, she had told her father, which impressed him, it seemed to her, more than anything she'd done.

A fast car traveling parallel to the tracks leaving Hamlet and heading north could have caught up with the train, but there were no parallel roads and the route to get to the mid-point involved going all directions but directly parallel.

Milly yelled this information about the pending accident to her mother, who leaned out the second-floor window of their big house. It would only be minutes before the wreck would either happen or be stopped. The trains would be traveling thirty miles an hour by the time they met. Three minutes had passed since the girl heard about it at the station. She had run home in two.

"People are going to try to stop it," she said.

Her father came onto the porch.

"They'll be crashing in a few minutes."

Cars whizzed by the house. The dirt roads boiled dust. Every kind of vehicle raced off in different directions, trying to figure out how best to get to the middle of the run.

There were fast Maxwells in the town, and a Kissel Kar, and a Saxon. One of Milly's neighbors drove a Cleveland and another had a Scripps-Booth. It seemed they were all on the road.

"Look at the cars," Milly said. "There's the Velie," she shouted. "It'll never catch them. It's so slow I can outrun it."

Emily ran past her husband and pulled Milly out of his arms.

She ran toward their own Auburn Beauty, which she had learned to drive a few months earlier. She backed the car onto the lawn and headed out already in second gear by the time the wheels skidded on the dirt road.

With Milly yelling out the window for everyone to get out of the way, and with Tips running behind them, they took off down the street, overtaking a Reo and a Rapid which was not living up to its name, as well as a Chalmers and an Overland, which had broken down on the side of the road. Milly, who knew every make and model by sight, called them out as they passed them.

"Around the Overland, Mommy."

Children ran after the cars and those who owned bicycles sped in the general direction everyone else seemed to be going. Milly saw one of her friends on his new Red Head Elgin King bike, and he was standing on the pedals and going for all he was worth.

"We're going to ride up the tracks and stop it," she screamed at him as they passed. "Don't hit my dog," she yelled, watching Tips about to catch up with them. "Stop, Mom. Let's get Tips in with us."

"We can't."

A group of men, four days away—like everyone else in the country—from the start of Prohibition, were in no condition to do any running and had come out of Happy Hooligan's to watch the commotion. The saloon had been named for a popular comic strip character. It had an amateurish painting of the character's face on the side of the building.

"That's Mrs. Austin," a man who did her yard work said. "Poor thing, look at her."

"She sure can drive," another man said.

Happy Hooligan looked like some of the men in front of the

saloon. He was a ragged man who had an optimistic outlook on whatever was happening, almost simple minded at times, and he was the exact opposite of his brother, Gloomy Gus.

"Where's she going?" someone asked the crowd as they watched her bump onto the tracks and head away, the car jiggling with one wheel between the rails and the other on the outside, but still up on the cross ties.

Emily was aware of her audience and had lucked into that very spot to make her dusty, billowing and wild-eyed debut for the men, lucked into it because she loved Happy Hooligan, and read it and the entire comic strips with Milly, the same as she had with Caroline and Milly, before the death.

"Well, darnation if she isn't going to try to catch that train from behind," one of the men said. "Now I wouldn't be a doing that," he added. "I would not."

Emily not only loved to read about Happy and his comical bad luck, but she loved his clothes, the tin can hat, the ragged sport coat with only one button, the knee-patched pants and the shoes with his toes coming out the ends.

"The little girl shouldn't be with her," the gardener said. "That's not safe."

Emily had daydreams of dressing up like a man and disappearing into the mayhem and freedom of a world where nothing was known about her and nothing was asked. She had daydreams of taking Milly along, and had worked out elaborate scenarios of the two of them sleeping in the grass, jumping on the cars, eating on the back steps of some good Samaritan's house, by the back door of a restaurant's kitchen, of being cared for, and at the same time, caring for herself in a way that was so simple and easy it was magical.

"That little girl's going to fall out that window," someone said as the car skittled along the cross ties and out of sight.

Except even in her daydreams she knew it was magical and unreal and that she could never do it with Milly, that it would be so clearly unsafe, and when she thought of that and couldn't dismiss it, she thought about putting on a play, or an act, just to wear the clothes, just to be that happily shabby.

"What'll they do if they do catch up," someone asked, now that the car was gone and they turned their attention to the dozen or so other vehicles and bicycles which passed by.

"I don't know. Flag down whoever's in the caboose," someone said.

The Auburn had torsion bars and coil springs and zipped along with a surprisingly smooth ride inside, while the wheels and tie rods and pivot arms took the beating. Cheaper vehicles, sprung like wagons, would have skidded into the rails and wrecked.

"Catch them, Mommy," Milly said. "We can do it."

Her mother had actually slowed down, sensing either they wouldn't be able to catch it, or not wanting to become involved in the collision herself, but continued on anyway because of how good it was to be out of the house, to be moving, to be steering the big car, to be in control of the long-hooded six-cylinder engine that shook her insides when she turned it loose, that felt like flying, as if she had jumped off something high and was, instead of falling, zooming downward like a hawk.

"Your father's right," she said to Milly. "Let's do pray for them. We should do that."

When trains had been first invented, the concept of speed was terrifying and unknown. It was the subject of debate just how fast the human body could travel before it deformed or altered in some way that nothing but fear could explain. At first it was thought that anything over thirty miles an hour would kill people. Emily had driven fifty recently, and that just a few years since the fear of speed was as powerful as sacrilege, as widely believed for its consequences as making a deal with the devil.

"What if they miss and the other train's coming right at us?" Milly asked. "What if they get on the other track over there and miss each other?"

Because the passenger trains were staffed with Negro porters, and because that was one of the highest paying jobs any black man could hold at the time, many people from north of Hamlet, in what would later be the Dobbins Heights Community, were aware of the pending disaster and had gathered together. They were outside their houses or at the station or in front of the hotels where other well-employed middle class Negroes worked as maids or white-jacketed waiters.

The trains crashed into each other so hard that Emily and Millicent, more than a half a mile away, felt the impact both in the air and along the ground, even more so as the rails conducted the concussion for miles in both directions.

"Oh," Milly said. "They hit."

Emily stopped her car. For another minute, but what seemed like much more, grinding and snapping sounds came from around the curve ahead of them as the train cars piled into each other and fell off the rails and tumbled into the ditch below the tracks. Trees popped off or uprooted and then mixed in with the interior of the cars as they fell over them, so that by the time Emily and Milly had driven down the embankment and parked in a patch of dewberries, both passengers and things that had once been passengers or parts of them were sticking out the broken windows and out of the peeled-back tops of the train cars along with the tree limbs, trunks and dirt.

Emily opened her door and had walked no more than a few paces when she fell. Her legs had given out from under her. She kneeled as if in prayer, trembling and weak the way she had felt when Caroline's casket had disappeared into the grave.

They walked below the elevated track. They stepped past some debris. People called for help. They heard lots of prayers. A man appeared in the window of a train car, looked directly at them, pulled himself through the opening, slid down the car like a serpent and then rolled down the embankment right to them. The man had deep, coal black skin but his lips were pale and his fingers were almost as white as theirs.

Emily got his head into her lap. He drifted away when she did, but she didn't think he was dead.

Milly knelt beside her mother and held the man's hand. Soon many of the town's people were there. They ferried the injured in their own cars back to the offices and homes of the three doctors. The man in Emily's lap died while she kept the insects away and blotted the dripping blood with her clothes.

Mr. Austin, who had been enlisted to help once the news was firm and it became the right thing to do, found them and checked the man's pulse and moved him out of his wife's lap.

The Negro community took the remaining passengers into their homes, churches and the schools, while they waited for the tracks to be cleared and for a special train the railroad was sending to return the passengers to Durham and take the injured to the hospitals in that bigger city.

"Did you think, did you imagine you would prevent that accident?" Mr. Austin asked Emily later that night when Millicent had finally been put to sleep with a dose of paregoric syrup, a camphorated tincture of opium, mixed into a cup of hot tea. "Whatever did you think you would or could do?"

He was in the study of the big house, and he was reading. He had a wall of books almost as high as the twelve-foot ceilings, and he read every night. He was, like many of the business and professional men in the town, like most of the lawyers, a scholar not associated with a university, simply a man who enjoyed knowledge and the process and virtue of learning, and who regularly met with his friends to discuss and debate.

"What did I think?" she asked.

(diary): There was a moment when I considered every thought not to mention the time spent considering everything I actually did. Now I don't. I love speed. I love the idea of wanton impulse. I might be encouraging Milly that way. I don't know, for certain. It might be wrong of me. What happens if I do? Will her life be worse than mine, more difficult because she's a free thinker, and then, if so, will her own children's lives be more difficult as the looseness is passed on and magnified, as it grows into something shrewd and billowing, not the muslin of my life.

There is a sweetness to security. I might be leading her astray. I can look back and see my grandmother who saw herself in Caroline, saw, like I've thought about so often, the particular inherited spirit that she felt was the distillation of herself, and I wish I could look forward and see where it leads, how it will grow like this town, building on itself, going wrong I suppose now and then, but continuing.

I wish I could see it and I hope to live long enough to watch Milly's life and the life of her sons and daughters and to be there to wish it well, to do what I can to continue this meditation not on the calculated soul, but on that other one, the one Caroline had, the one I found, the one Milly now has. Don't know what to call it. Not innocence. It's the place we go after we've lost that, but want to return. It's that. It's there. It's where I am after I had my children but understood I never wanted anymore, after I married but understood I couldn't, anymore, be myself, who I said I was. It's out there at the end of speed, at the impulse where the magneto sparks, where the electricity runs out the sockets and across the floor and up my feet.

What did I think I could do? he asked. I don't know. I simply had to go, had to try, had to take Milly along, had to. The deaths did not remind me of Caroline. I'm trying to be happier for her. To be good, helpful, and alive.

Tomorrow we'll go, as a family, because we are, to the new soda shop, a Main Street palace of onyx and marble, with more than 300 flavors of ices and sodas and tonics, a cool and sparkling temple with a counter as long as a ship. It'll be like a voyage to a new place, and Milly's eyes will glow, and it will be, for a moment, that place where nothing is wrong and everything, anything, is possible, a little miracle of change in the mouth, on the tongue, on the fingertips, the icy glass of magical surprise, and everyone is happy.

CHAPTER 4

Mr. Austin lost money before the crash of 1929. He lost more in that one notorious week, and continued to lose during the worst of the decline, which lasted until 1933. His tenants couldn't pay their rent. All the banks in Hamlet failed.

Everything had a cycle that affected the next person, who, until that time, might have been financially sound. One person can't pay another, who then can't pay someone else because he wasn't paid, and the third, owed by the second, can't pay the fourth, because he wasn't paid, and so on.

Emily was a grandmother in 1933. Milly had married one of the men who managed the family's dewberry farm, and their daughter, Anita, who would be Ellie's grandma, was now seven. The farm was up for sale and Milly and her family lived in the big house with Emily and Mr. Austin.

At the end of May there was a lot of social activity. Milly and her husband Teddy were chaperones at the Junior Senior Banquet. The menu was lush for the hard times of the day. It was pork roast, creamed potatoes, hot biscuits, chicken salad, saltines, pickles, iced tea, gelatin, cake and mints.

On Monday evening the entire family attended the annual Inter-Society Contest at the Opera House. The program began with the high school chorus singing *Come Genial Spring* by Gribal. Emily wrote in her diary.

There is a Tom Thumb wedding next week. These have become popular and the children participating get excited about it. It's for charity, for the Widows' and Oprhans' fund. The families with money have already been to the Elite Millinery Shop and have actually been buying dresses from Paris and New York. I am to presume that they will not be going broke like we are, or that they merely think they're protected and beyond such a fate. There's a lot going on for charity now. So sad the other night when there was the Father and Son Supper for all the men and boys in town. Any man who had no son could borrow an extra one from a man who had more than one, and any boy who had no father could borrow a man.

Mr. Austin was volunteered for poor little Buster Ellis, who was told his father had died but of course we all know that he left town before the boy was born, never to be heard from again. It's a sorry family, coarse and mean, but maybe someone in it will rise up. I bought the boy a suit, which cost me $4.98. After I had it delivered, I realized that was wrong and should have given them the money instead. The Ellis' are poor as the Negroes who live near them. The Negro families are having their own event out at their own school.

Later.

I tried to sleep but am awake again. I'm so sick. I won't tell anyone. Christian manhood and scathing honorary arm-chair moralists talk about love. When it isn't lustful it is like duty and perfunctory goodness. I never mastered it, or him, like some few women do. I only wanted to be with my girls. I don't even remember ever having what I read about so often, which is what they call the flame of love, or hate. I never hated anyone. I hated death and suffering and the difficulty of believing. If my husband has no money, then I have no money, because what I had became his and now that's gone, then what? I don't think we have any money left.

I thought about Mrs. Rosser recently, the nurse. I wrote a lot about her when Caroline was sick. She's dead. No one told me. I would have gone to the funeral. She'd moved to Laurinburg. She was good to Caroline, and good to me. I needed her, too. Now she's dead. We loved words. We loved to play with them. We wanted to make something that was meaninglessly friviol. A word like that. Friviolly, we laughed.

I have this entire life inside me that I suppose no one knows about, knows all of it, only the little parts that have spilled out. I guess it's the part of me that Milly loves, that we share. That I gave to her. That she'll give to her daughter Anita. That we'll pass down as the only inheritance we have, now that the money's gone. And that will be good. Because it sustains.

CHAPTER 5

In 1952 Anita worked in the Buttercup Ice Cream plant on Bridges Street alongside the tracks near the station. This was the building that would become the chicken plant.

"I'm here," Anita said as she entered the cool tile building. "What are we making today?"

The technology of refrigeration had changed from the end of the nineteenth to the early part of the twentieth century. Steam engines had been used to drive the refrigeration units. Once there was sufficient electricity, small electric motors had to be invented to turn the units, everything getting smaller and more efficient all the time. Until then, though, the steam engines sat outside the buildings liked derailed locomotives. Flat belts running on pulleys went off in many directions and seemingly without plan, the way a person's body would look if he or she had fifteen arms coming off the same torso, all moving at once. The belts ran everything that had to move, every gear, pulley, pump or conveyor.

"I hope it's fudge ripple," she said.

The steam-driven systems vibrated. Leaks within the refrigeration units were a problem, and since the chemical instrument for removing the heat from the air was sulfur dioxide or ammonia, the leaks were dangerous. The first successfully sealed system was invented in France in the 1890s by a Cistercian monk, and that system was then licensed and sold in the U.S. by the Johns Manville company and manufactured by General Electric.

"If it's fudge ripple, let me be the one to clean up the mixer," Anita said to her friends as she walked through the plant on the way to the room where she worked. "Do let me."

Later, units using methyl chloride were invented, such as the Autofrigor. Those units had a problem with their own heat melting their own parts. They were replaced by the Savage Mercury Refrigeration unit, which was based on the principals of the Archimedes Screw. Mercury was swirled in slugs up an inclined, rotating screw and isobutene and methyl chloride was compressed between the mercury slugs. This system was manufactured by the Savage Arms Company, which also made shotguns.

"I wish Louise could be here with me at the end of the day," Anita said, speaking of her daughter, who would be Ellie's mother. "She'd love to clean up if it involved licking that sweet fudge and vanilla."

"Bring her," her supervisor said. "Let's get all our children in here to clean up. One licks, one cleans, and then they switch off. Anyone who wants to can."

In the early days, the Buttercup plant made ice cream from blocks of butter that were brought in by rail in refrigerated cars. There was no problem with resupplying the refrigerated cars with ice once in Hamlet, or shipping out the finished ice cream in five and ten gallon containers, because the largest ice plant in the Southeast was located there, built specifically for supplying the railroads. The ice plant produced 100 tons of ice a day.

"We've done it before. I think it'll be fine."

The blocks of butter were mixed with powdered milk. There were two basic mixes made in the plant, the white mix and the chocolate mix. The mixer man, who was Anita's friend, had arrived that day at four A.M. to get the mix started. Once it was begun, the plant had to stay in full operation until it went through the processes to the finished, frozen product. Everyone had to pitch in no matter what was needed so that the batch, moving from one stage to another, continued smoothly.

"What am I making today, anyway? Is it Neapolitan?" Anita asked.

Before reaching the cooling vat, the mixture was pumped to the homogenizer, where it was forced under 2,500 pounds of pressure through a small tipped cone. The cones were like a megaphone in that the mix entered the wide end of the cone and was forced out the other end, which was so small it broke up the fat globules and made the mix, if seen as a collection of random clumps of different sizes and shapes, all the same, so that a ladled sample taken anywhere would look and feel and pour alike, all smooth and consistent. The trick then was to keep it that way.

From the homogenizing process the mixture went into the cooling vat, which lowered the temperature of the mix to 38 degrees by means of a heat exchanger.

"Butter pecan," Anita said. "How wonderful."

This 38-degree mixture now moved toward Anita. It was not even vanilla yet. It was flavorless. She added the sugar and pecans and flavorings and the temperature was reduced to 21 degrees.

"What molds are we using?" she asked when she saw a stack of trays like cupcake pans only bigger and made from wood. "It's for a big party?" she asked.

"I think so," someone said.

Some of the mix then stopped off in a room where a dozen women wearing white smocks and hats received it in a long open tray. The remainder was put in five-gallon steel or cardboard containers and moved to the hardening room, where it would be reduced to 20 degrees below zero.

Because ammonia was used in the pipes in that big walk-in freezer, and because ammonia under pressure was 40 degrees below zero, it was simply a matter of time before the constantly replenished pressurized ammonia forced everything in the hardening room down toward its own temperature. Even warm bodies in there briefly would freeze hard as ice cream.

Pipes ran below and above shelves. Frost followed the flow of the ammonia like cool, silvery paint, as if the pipes were painting and repainting themselves. Skin stuck to these pipes not as if it had been grabbed, but the way something would be snatched and eaten.

"It's for the Rotary Club," a woman said. "Not a party."

"Not the Rotary," another woman said. "It's for the Lions Club. And the Lionesses. They're serving the boys tonight."

The supervisor came back in the room and the women gathered around.

"We can all leave when the forms are filled and hardened and the mixtures are finished running, and get our kids for the cleanup. They agreed it was fine. But we have to do it in a hurry."

Every day, before anyone could go home, and not just this day, every piece of the machinery, the vats, the hoses, the mixers, the beaters, the stirrers, the pumps, the cones and fins and tables and cans and cups and spoons and ladles, everything had to be taken apart, and cleaned and dried so that not only was there nothing to go sour or bad overnight, but all the previous day's flavorings and additives would be gone so as not to make imperfect the flavors run the next day.

"But?" Anita asked.

"But what?"

"What are the tree shapes for? Who's that for? The thousand of those?"

"Think about what flavor we're running today."

"Butter pecan? I don't know."

"Trees, Anita. Think trees."

"Peach growers?"

"Nope."

"Timber merchants group?"

"No."

"The pecan growers?"

"And we are dipping them in chocolate, as well."

Anita's mother had never worked outside the home. She had not lived to see Louise running around town and riding her bicycle with her hair flying behind her and her jeans scuffed in the knees and her face tanned and freckled. She was so much like her great aunt Caroline, who she often heard about in stories, especially stories told while sitting in their 1949 Chevrolet, parked across the street from the grand old house that had once been in their family, but was now a funeral home where Louise's daughter, Ellie McCorkle, would, in 1991, be spending some time soon after the fire, in one of the upstairs' rooms.

PART II

On a Chicken Wing and a Prayer

CHAPTER 6

Can't See It From My House

On Friday morning, in 1991, just before the start of the Labor Day weekend, someone from Capital Food phoned Central Carolina Hydraulics and ordered a hose for a cooking unit.

"Can we get them a replacement for that fryer by late today?" the person at C.C.H. asked the shop worker.

"I don't know," he said. "I suppose I can get to it."

"Get it to me by noon."

"Yeah, okay."

"Have to have it."

Separate spools of yellow, red and black hose hung on galvanized iron pipes. Fumes from an idling delivery truck sucked upward into the cool air returns and the raw, metallic taste of carbon monoxide settled into coffee cups and Dr. Peppers. A mouse hip-hopped across the floor with a chocolate cookie in its mouth. A man threw a rubber hammer at it. The driver in the idling delivery truck remained in the cab. He unwrapped a pork tenderloin biscuit and peeled a sliver of fat from around the edge.

"Who was that?" the shop worker's partner, Puddin, asked and then yelled across the room, "Hey buddy. Get that truck out of here or shut it off."

The driver flicked the peel of fat out the window of his truck and bit into the biscuit.

"That was *Get-it-to-me-by-noon*," the shop worker said, still holding his end of the new phone in his oily fingers which had, in less than a month, caused the smooth white handset to look like it had been dipped in chocolate ice cream.

"She's always saying that. I wonder if she knows she says it every time."

The man who'd thrown the hammer walked past Puddin with a Jolt Cola in his hand and told him he had a headache the size of Pennsylvania.

"I'm dying," he said to Puddin. "I wish somebody would drill a hole in my skull. Right here."

He took four ibuprofen tablets. Phones rang, metal clanged, motorized shears hummed and snipped, and a sheet of paper blew into the air and then floated like a kite in a downward spiral. A steel drawer with too much in it jammed and the man searching for the fitting jerked it and let it fall to the floor. It hit so loudly everyone went silent, as if they'd been slapped.

"Good morning," the man said. Nobody laughed.

"I doubt she knows she asks it every time," the first man answered, catching the conversation back up after the crash. "Get it to me by noon."

"We ought to change her name. Call her Gitumee Bunoon."

"How come they don't understand something? If I have these orders to do today and some of them are hers, are Gitumee's, and she keeps calling with more added in, how'm I supposed to do these?"

Practical jokes were a regular event in the shop, especially antics that involved the female clerical staff.

Leaving a black or diamond patterned reinforced hose in someone's drawer or under a desk and watching him or her jump and yell, "Snake!" was always fun, but having a long black hose creep out of one of the shop workers unzipped fly was what they all dreamed and talked about doing.

"I got a good one I been thinking about for Miss Bunoon," the first shop worker said. "Her desk is right beside the wall. Right in that exact spot where those two pieces join."

"Right there," Puddin said.

"I'm going to run a line right through the bottom of that wall and have it come out at the foot of her desk, aiming up."

"Uh huh."

"Then, I'm going to hook it to the compressor and about the time she walks by, I'm going to blow a hundred and twenty pounds compressed air right up her crotch."

"I know it'll be the first time she felt anything moving in between them legs in a long, long time."

"Shit, I wouldn't have it on a plate, for free," another said. "Not for nothing."

"Me, neither," another one, who had been longing for her and dreaming about her, fantasizing about her for a year, said. "Not me. Lord no."

At eleven, the woman they now called Gitumee buzzed back to the shop and discovered the line wasn't ready yet.

"What kind of fryer is it?" Puddin asked, having deduced from what he heard they would have to look it up themselves.

"A Stein."

"Steinway Grand Pianos and fryers," he said. He had a habit

of making any name or word bigger than it was. He punched in numbers on the dirty keyboard in front of him. "Yeah, I believe I seed it right here."

"Any damn thing'll work. It's just a hose."

"Just a hose. Hosay can you see the number to be," he sang as he scrolled along the list of parts and models.

"I reckon I know what it is anyway. Isn't it the same one they got last time? And how come they can't make it up theirselves?"

"I wouldn't work in a chicken plant for all the chickens I could steal out the back door."

"Got it yet?"

"Those chickens just fly through the place," he said and went up and down the list so many times his partner shut his eyes and looked away. "In one end and out the other before you could fry an egg."

"Have you found her?"

"I flounder, but then I lobster," Puddin said

"Damn computers," the first one said, leaning over his co-worker's shoulder and trying to see what had happened. "There isn't a letter left on that keyboard that isn't smudged. You suppose the folks what made the computer ever figured out the people using them aren't all sitting in offices wearing white gloves?"

"I can fix that," he said and took out a knife and carved an arrow on the button he guessed had originally had that symbol.

The air compressor cycled on. The screen blinked, went blank and then came back with warnings and bar graphs peeling across it like bullets fired at them.

"Danger is my middle name," Puddin said, content to sit at the screen while the computer rebooted. "I'll just start again. It's almost lunch. I have a hunch. And I don't want brunch. Just a bunch of lunch."

"Forget it. I'll make up what I think it is. It's all one-inch hose, anyway."

"How long is it? Did you see before you lost it?"

"Longer than yours, not as long as mine."

"Let's make it plenty long."

"Why did the chicken cross the road halfway?"

"What?" the first worker asked, starting to cut and clamp together the quick-attach fittings onto the hose. "Half what?"

"She wanted to lay it on the line."

"Uh huh."

"They don't have quick couplers on that thing."

"They don't?"

The first man cut off those fittings and got the threaded style, measured the flexible hose and then made it two-and-a-half feet longer than what he thought it was. He set up, in an orderly manner on a steel-topped table, the configuration of the threaded couplings that would allow it to connect to what was already on the fryer.

"I'll take it up front when you get it ready," Puddin said. "Need any help?"

"Who's driving the afternoon deliveries?"

"Alphon-so-what, I reckon."

"So-what's driving? Tell him if it ain't the right one, to tell them a good man can make anything work. Have him to tell that boy over there that."

"It looks good to me."

"Good enough for government work."

"Can't see it from my house," the first man said and handed it over and started out the back door. "I'll pick you up around front, for lunch."

"KFC today?"

"Can't see it from my house," Puddin said as he walked toward the front of the building. "Hosay can you see it from my house, no speekee Engliss, See-nor, See-nor-ita," he continued on, making up words and sounds and whistling as he went through the doors, thinking about the work not at all, but mimicking, in his own way, as he had been all day long, W.C. Fields, having seen him the evening before on a cable channel. "Not fit for man nor beast," he said.

"About time," she said.

"Lunch time is about my time," he said and went out the front and got in the truck with his buddy.

CHAPTER 7

———————————————————————————

Carly played outside with her friend.

It was 3 P.M. and 94 degrees. The sun was softened and gauzy and buttery in the blue sky. The humidity was high; breathing felt heavy, like trying to inhale warm water. Asphalt parking lots were close to liquid. Tires adhered to the tar while barefoot children danced a sizzling jig.

"Sit in that box," she told him.

The lawn was a trimmed, wild salad of grass and weeds which had turned brown and crisp like fried noodles. Lois, Carly's mother, had mowed it too short the day before so that at ground level, viewed sideways, the way a child would look across the lawn while lying flat, it looked singed, like some man's fifties flattop haircut that had been scorched with a flame.

"I not going to sit in that bock," the friend said.

Two raised flower beds, like heaved graves, were at the edge of the yard where it met the house, and the remains of early blooming daffodils, yellow heads on faded green stems, leaned toward the ground, thin, melting bodies, starved and wasted. Week by week a wild rose bush took over one end of the house and a bird's nest, now empty, lodged within the thorns. Beside the bush, on the ground, a pair of snips had been struck by the mower. The rubber cushioned handles were cut with a slice, the gash so deep it went to the bone, the metal beneath.

"That bock feel greasy," he added.

"That's wax," Carly said.

Lois worked at the chicken plant and earned $220 per week. Her house rented for $300 per month, not counting utilities. Out of the paycheck, 15% went to taxes and social security, which left her with a take home of $748 per month. After the rent, $448 remained for utilities, food, gas, auto insurance, repairs, clothes, medical care and the rest. The company offered minimal health insurance, but it paid little in benefits, cost too much and if you had made claims, she'd heard, the premiums went up.

"Wax?"

"Put it on your head," she told him.

The children had eleven boxes in the yard. Lois and her neighbor, Evelyn, had gotten them out of the compactor at the plant before they were crushed for recycling. The boxes normally held 60 pounds of frozen chicken breasts, tenderloins or nuggets which people called fingers. At cookouts or volunteer fire department suppers, deep-fried chicken fingers were popular.

Lois had cut the grass with the new lawnmower she'd bought for $98. It came with the wheels set low and she didn't have a wrench and screwdriver to set them higher. More expensive mowers had tabs for adjustment.

Years ago, yardmen walked the streets of Hamlet with cans of gasoline tied to the handles of mowers. Most of those yardmen came from Dobbins Heights, where Lois lived. Dobbins was originally a community called North Yard because it was north of the

Seaboard Air Line Railroad. It had been mostly African Americans who lived there, many of them employed by the railroad in good jobs. It was still a community primarily of black families.

"I'll put one on my head, too," Carly said.

Dobbins Heights became an incorporated area, that is, an actual town with a government and taxes and services, in 1984. It had its own volunteer fire department. This department had been formed in 1974, because it was felt by people like Arthur 'Lumbee' Farver, Lois' uncle, that fires in their community were answered late and begrudgingly by the Hamlet department.

Lois was a single mother with dreams of a better life for herself and her daughter. She did not want to be associated with the stigma of the weedy yard. She had hauled the mower home in the trunk of her '79 Caprice. The handles folded. The trunk was deep. She had hurt herself lifting it out, and could, even now sitting on the porch in front of a window that had a box fan fitted into the opening, feel the numbness down her leg.

She felt this same twang, like an electrical shock, when she bent forward working at the processing tables at Capital.

"We going to be bock monsters?"

Her house had one bathroom, a kitchen, a breakfast room, two bedrooms and a den. It was covered on the outside with hard asbestos shingle siding, a painter's favorite, as it never peeled or warped and held paint like glue. The front yard was divided by a buckled paved walkway. The driveway was dirt and grass. The backyard was continuous with all the other yards on the street, broken only by plantings and Lowe's western cedar fence panels nailed in eight-foot sections to four-by-four posts.

Some dogs wandered freely. Some were chained. They barked

incessantly and ran bare-ground paths in circles around trees and tipped over dog houses. Some were held by stakes driven into the sandy soil, and they wound themselves up in a fury of confined madness. Cats learned, to the inch, just how far a chain allowed a dog's movement and strolled haughtily and with enraging intent just beyond reach.

"I know what. You get under this one with me," Carly said. "We pretend we're at the beach, under an umbrella."

A white papery nest had been built on one inside corner of the porch ceiling. Wasps flew against it all day long, while on the fascia of the same porch, big, black carpenter bees buzzed and dived and flew in and out holes they had drilled through the trim board and into the framing. Two guard bees shot toward everything that came within range, hovered, and then returned to their posts. All day the wasps and the big bees tended their territory, workers of the insect world, doing their own jobs.

The golf courses, public and private, were full this Labor Day, from one end to the other. The town of Hamlet was near Pinehurst and Southern Pines, legendary golfing resorts from the early days of the sport to the present.

The nearest Lois had ever gotten to a golf ball was when she walked past a display of them in a hardware store. She didn't know a nine iron from pig iron, a driver from a drover, and the name 'sand trap' sounded more like a description of her life than a maddening place to play a shot in a game that seemed, to her, had she been questioned, beyond foolish.

"I'm going to work with my mom tomorrow. I'm going to skip school. I know how to fry chicken," Carly said.

The outside of the box over the children's head was hot to the touch. Inside, they were in their own dark, cool world except for the sliver of sunlight that came through a slit. The light cut across Carly's cheek like a white scar on her dark skin.

"You just drop the breaded piece on the chain and it takes it right into the grease," she said. "And I not skipping school. I got permission. And your momma's not in Philadelphia," she added, tilting the box so she could see what she'd just heard happening outside.

"She is, too."

"Then who's that?" she asked, and pointed to a woman standing near a car that was slowly driving off. "Who's that?"

Carly's nails were painted five different colors. Her thumbs were red, forefingers yellow, middle finger pink, and then the other two green and gold. She had pierced ears and her hair was braided tightly and tied with ribbons. She wore pale brown shorts and a tee-shirt with the words "Holiness Baptist VBS" on it.

Her mother had on knee-length shorts and a cotton/polyester blouse which she had bought along with her daughter's clothes just the week before while getting ready for the school year, at Wal-Mart in Rockingham, the nearest location. Lois was five-feet-five and weighed 170 pounds. On Friday night she had baked chicken filets and smothered them in Hidden Valley Ranch Dressing once they were done and on the plates. She had about two dozen more filets in the freezer compartment of her old Roper refrigerator. Evelyn had given her the meat, having gotten it somehow out of the plant in whatever way Lois did not want to know. She had given it to Lois as thanks for looking after her son all the times she needed that help.

CHAPTER 8

Jay missed the wall hook. The phone fell. The white plastic door to the battery compartment popped into the air. It landed in a sink full of dishes and sunk beneath the water.

"Not my day," he said to Lizzy while he tried to replace the part which would not go back on. "The tab's broken. I'll tape it."

They worked at Capital Foods.

"You can fix anything."

"Buck don't think so."

"Don't talk like him."

They were both 27 years old. They lived in a 14-by-80 manufactured house in one of the nicest mobile home parks in the Hamlet area. They had 1,120 square feet, with three bedrooms, two baths, a bay window, bubble-globed lights recessed in the ceiling and shiny, maple-decaled cabinets.

"Lois and I were talking about Buck the other day," she said. "About him and all the bosses. How come," she asked while leaning out the doorway and listening for the sound of either of their two children, "they got to treat everyone like they're idiots?"

Lizzy had been on unpaid leave since before she had the baby.

She was going back Tuesday when her ex-step-mother, who she paid $20 a day, would be looking after both children.

"He knows if I learn what he learns, I'd have his job. I think that's why he puts me on things I'll mess up the first time. I always get them right the second."

"Look at the sun," she said. They looked through the window and then walked outdoors. "It's a lovely color. I've never seen that before."

In the previous week, in the Gobi Desert, a nearly cataclysmically huge sandstorm had been drawn straight up into the sky by unusual meteorological forces. The sand traveled in the atmosphere across the Pacific Ocean.

"It's so rich. It's beautiful," Lizzy said.

It was visible from space, a yellow river above the earth. It was reported by the few lonely astronauts circling at the time, and photographs were sent down. The sand from the Gobi was now east of North Carolina, and had colored the sun the tone and texture of butterscotch almond cream.

Lizzy and Jay had lost their better paying, $8.75 an hour textile jobs a couple of years ago when their mill, which made tee shirts, closed and reopened in Mexico. The workers there made $1.50 an hour with no benefits and were thrilled to have it.

Because many other textile operations had closed about the same time, Jay and Lizzy had gone to Job Services to look for new work and to see about getting unemployment compensation while they waited. They were given a slip with the name and address of Capital Foods. They were told to take the jobs if there were any open. They were told that they couldn't collect their unemployment money if jobs were available and they failed to accept the work.

After they accepted their jobs, they found out that most of the people working there had been laid off and had been sent to the chicken plant with the same threat of take it or else.

Lizzy set her cup in the sink. The kitchen was part of the big open room that extended more than a third of the way down the home, creating a 14-by-30-foot area, bigger than any room either had grown up with in their own childhood mobile homes.

Jay was six feet tall and his wife was five-one. The height of the conveyor belts caused her arms to ache as she had to reach up to do her job, but for people closer to six feet, that same table height caused their backs to hurt.

"They ought to fret about the carcasses they get sent to them. They're all bunged up before they even get to us. Discolored and punched up."

"I bought some wings at the deli at Lowes Food the other day, and the bones were broken just like the ones we get. Poor birds."

He, like all the maintenance employees, made more than the line workers. His gross pay was close to $14,000 a year and his wife's, like most of the people in her department, was about $11,000. The mortgage payment, which, on mobile homes were set up similar to automobile payments, was $350 a month, the lot rent was $125, the utilities were about $100 a month, and the health insurance for the whole family was another $500 a month. After taxes, that totaled more than Lizzy's take home, and Jay's income made two car payments of $250 a month each, which left $400, after taxes, for food, childcare and everything else.

Jay's father drove up in his Silverado, came in and told him about a job opening at the L'eggs factory where he worked.

"When do I apply?" Jay asked.

They walked to the children's room. The sixteen-day-old girl,

Destiny, slept on her back under a cotton blanket. Her lips were puckered and ever so slightly moving, as if she was thinking about nursing, which she'd done for the first week, and then been weaned to the bottle so Lizzy could return to work. Beside her, on a new single bed with chairs put against the side, was her brother, Silas, not quite so sound asleep at eight-thirty in the morning but drooling a little puddle, just outside his mouth, onto the pillow.

"Is there anything for me?" Lizzy asked.

"There's usually something for the women," Jay said. "Right, Dad?"

"Maybe."

"So when should I apply? Who do I see?"

"Come on in tomorrow. If you can. Both of you."

"I can't in the morning. I know we got some work to do right off. A hose came in late Friday and we didn't do it."

"Let's skip work and go apply," Lizzy said.

"I have to help fix that hose or they'll shut the fryer down."

"Then let's leave early and go apply."

CHAPTER 9

Ellie McCorkle was like the driver of a speeding car that had lost traction and was sliding sideways down the road. She had not yet crashed, but she wasn't sure she knew how to straighten out. She was sideways to life. She could see where she was supposed to go, but it felt like the steering wheel had disconnected and she was turning it this way and that without effect.

She was 20, and had been born in 1971, the year her mother Louise met, married and left her father.

I am a girl from Nofunland, she thought, where it is cold and dark all the time. I am a Nofunlander, yah, this must be true.

Her life had recently become a curious adventure, which she was keeping to herself at that moment.

Yah, an adventure in Nofunland, maybe?

Oh yah, I must go north and be cold. I must leave our little hamlet, she thought just as Ricky touched her arm and leaned across the bottom of the bed and put his face close to hers.

"I'm kind of possessed by a negative force field today," she said.

"I could tell."

"I wish I could tell."

"What?" he added, trying to figure out where she was going.

"Wish you could tell something? Tell me something?"

"Yes," she said, lying across the bottom of the bed with her feet off one end, toes pointing down, and her hands drawing doodles in the dust on the floor off the other end, "maybe. And maybe not."

"I'm listening."

"De sire-een, she don't sire no more," she said.

"You're a siren, that's for sure. You call for me and I come to you and then you speed away."

I yam the me and the not me. I yam to go to north, it is true.

"Sorry. I know I do that," she said.

Desire under the elms kept running through her mind, thinking that all the elm trees had died from the disease and plague, desire under what elms? She kept hearing that phrase over and over. There wasn't an elm tree in Hamlet any bigger or thicker than her gorgeous but tragically skinny boyfriend. He was so oddly boney that his body could, sideways in the right light, look like an insect's.

"Hated——to——tell——you," she said, drawing the words slowly like she found herself doing this evening to much of what she said. "But, like the warning says, do not attempt this girl on your own."

"I'm listening," he said

"Desire under the elms," she said.

"There's something wrong with desire?"

"Splendor in the grass," she whispered, intentionally again obscuring what she said to him, and then wanted to cry, imagining herself Natalie Wood, somehow transferring that feeling of longing and grief and loss to her own life, weeping last night with her mom while they watched that movie on cable, both of them crying and then laughing at themselves for crying so hard. She tried to remember how Ms. Wood had recited that poem and what it said, and wanted to do it herself, right then, and rush out of the room.

"Splinter what?"

"Splen-door," she said. "As in, the way life should be."

I love you, she whispered, almost like a thought but with just enough air so that it became the faintest of words.

She had said it to see how it would sound at the time, that night, right then, and if she could even say it out loud. She had enjoyed saying it all her life, as a child to her mother and father, to her friends as they gushed it back to her, just the thought of it was inspiring, like a prayer. She had practiced saying it to boys later on, almost, she sometimes thought, creating the relationship so she could try it out. It was something that needed to be said. It was like a reverse drug, something that needed to go out instead of come in. I love you. She and all her girl friends had been made to know that these three words must be said. To not say them was to fail. They went out into the world, then, looking for someone to say them to.

The act of being what you knew and felt like you were inside, even if you hadn't lived up to it or no one else had ever seen it, was a trick that was hard to do. It was a plate spinning act where two dozen discs were all whirling on separate stilts, all the plates making a sound that seemed to be like flying, like air in motion as you, the spinner, she thought, kept them going and flew out of your life.

"You know, girls are raised on a diet of goodness and reflection, and then, only later, do we get stupid."

Ricky had a refined and understated manliness and good looks, from the neck up, anyway, more like a man from an old movie, like the man who'd played opposite Clark Gable in *Gone with the Wind*, Leslie Howard, she thought, that's who Ricky looked like, sensitive and intelligent and thoughtful. A Frank Capra character. Jimmy Stewart. That was who he was supposed to be. That was who she was supposed to make him be. The good man in her life.

How a man looked, she thought, was all about how you wanted him to look. Women created themselves, or their friends did, or most of all, their mothers helped in the creation, imagining somehow that a girl in Hamlet, North Carolina, could be the next Ava Gardner, who had, after all, grown up not far from there and in similar circumstances.

Men weren't grown like orchids to look a certain way, to be hot-housed or blooming, their arms opened like inviting petals, cheeks as soft as puffs of pollen; they just were, and women figured out what it was those men were. They spent the time and effort to figure that out.

"We could read," he said. "We could do that if it suits you better. I've got a book by Randall Jarrell you'd like. We could read each other parts of it."

"Parts of it," she echoed.

"It's called *Pictures from an Institution*. I think you'll love it."

"Trying to tell me something?"

"No. Forget the title. It's ironic. You'll love the words, the language. The woman, the main character. It's so fifties. It's you."

This, she thought, was his effort to connect better to her, but she couldn't fall into the opening. She had told him she liked Jarrell and now he'd gotten a book and of all things, it was the same book she had bought in Raleigh a month before, but had yet to read it. It should be, she thought, that she would love him for this. That she would say yes.

"Okay. Let's do that. Later."

"Later would be better. I need to run home. Mom's made some cookies for me to take back to school."

He went to the university in Chapel Hill. Ellie had not gotten in, and didn't have the money, had she gotten in.

"I love her cookies," she said.

Ricky left her alone in his friend's one-room apartment. The walls were gray and dim and hazy. The ceiling had 12-inch squares of formerly white, textured cardboard-like tile with many small holes punched in it. It dated from when people believed that type of finish would soundproof a room. It was as gray as the walls except for a clean, bright ring in the very center where the light fixture had come loose. It hung by its wires, revealing, in that startling white ring, how clean and almost perfect, relative to what was around it now, the idea and intentions for that room had been at one time.

She stared at the color that had been revealed by the collapse of the light, at the perfect circle that had been made by the base of the fixture pressed tightly against the resilient tile, and as she studied it, almost hypnotized by the sight in a way that felt pleasurable, so focused and powerfully connected her eyes seemed like they were pulling outward from their sockets, lost in the unexpected perfection and appearance of the pure and the white and the clearly defined circumference, she felt herself ascending weightless, floating up to the ceiling and into the tiny, white arc almost as if she were stoned, or on mushrooms, which she was not.

She was not only clean of chemical alteration, she had not even eaten anything all day, preferring the sense of emptiness in her stomach, the weakness in her muscles, the dryness in her mouth and how her heart beat faster so that she could, it seemed to her when she focused on it, feel her blood flowing, actually flowing, especially through her belly and legs, a hot, nearly erotic sensation.

Not yet having blinked, so that her eyes went dry and burned, she continued floating upward toward the ceiling until, just as unexpectedly as she had begun, she stopped. A little head with feelers and armament and pincers appeared in the dead center where the wires went into the attic space, and a beetle crawled into view and then onto one of the wires, slipped ever so slightly and then balanced there a moment until the door suddenly opened and slammed shut. Ricky came back and the beetle dropped onto the bed.

Ellie did a back flip and rolled off the bed in the opposite direction of the fierce looking beetle. She looked for the creature which had appeared, as close to her face as it had been, as big as an animal rather than an insect. She saw it scoot under a pillow.

She was five-feet-eight-inches, jogged three miles every other day, had a short haircut that was distinctive and retro and she wore clothes from past times, fifties and sixties dresses and scarves and blouses, grandma's hats with veils and buttons and flowered pins, Boy Scout shirts with all the ribbons and medals, delivery man shirts with "Bob" or "Scottie" on the nametag, anything, everything. She looked unlike anyone else she knew and she had made herself that way.

"What just happened?" Ricky asked.

She patted him on the shoulder and then spun him around so he was looking away from the door and as she whirled him toward the bed and the wall, she gave him a push, just enough to tilt him off balance. Before he could recover, she was out the door.

She cruised through Dobbins Heights and by Lois' house, briefly interested in this woman without knowing she would ever see her again the way she sometimes saw people and wanted to know them or talk to them, but saw the woman and the little girl on the porch, saw the child on what probably was, she thought, her mother's lap, and she wanted to stop and talk to them.

She did not stop, but drove on to Gwen's house. It was half of an older duplex in dark brick. She tapped on the narrow, amber-colored, pebbly glass panel in the front door. Lights were on, and music played, and her friend finally heard her knocking.

They sat in Early American-style matching platform rockers with a matching table between them and across the room, a long couch that had the same cozy Americana fabric.

"My dad called," Ellie said.

"Uh oh."

"He's in a mess."

"And if he's in trouble, you're in trouble."

"He needs money. He won't say why. I got to do something about it."

"Of course."

"It seemed bad. I can't tell the man no."

"Right."

"Which is what you were thinking just then."

"And for sure your mom doesn't want to hear about it."

"He only tells me his troubles. He's part of my ongoing adventure."

"How much?"

"A lot. He has no money whatsoever."

"Where's he living?"

"At a motel."

"He does have a sweet nature about him. Poor thing."

"Poor sweet old drunk thing. I paid for a week yesterday. For him. With my credit card. That filled it up."

"If you want to come to the chicken plant for a few weeks and work like hell, you could make a lot of money. There's nowhere else close by you can work. No one's hiring."

"Could I work two shifts?"

"What about school?"

She was taking a fashion design course at the local community college.

"I don't know. I can figure something out. I'll figure it out."

To make everything just that much crazier, that much more impossible and full of bad luck, she was pregnant. She'd stopped the pill because she thought it was making her sore and sick. She didn't ask the doctor about it.

She didn't want a baby. She didn't want to have it. She didn't want to give it away or keep it. She didn't want to get rid of it. She didn't want to tell Ricky. She didn't want anything to do with it. She wanted everything to do with it. She didn't know what to do.

She'd been making other plans for her life. She had backed into a pole a few months ago, crumpled her bumper, didn't tell the insurance company, didn't fix it, and realized it was the kind of thing her father would have done. The crumpled bumper then became a metal and plastic mantra, an om of fix me fix you. She quit drinking so much and made plans for her future.

She thought she might make a film, or a documentary, or write a book about her friend Byrum. An oral history. Something about him, something to do with him. She had even given him a tape recorder to capture his life and his amazing and strange world, and the way his mind or what was left of it worked and the way he used words, and then, in one week, her father had called with his news just days after she had found out she was pregnant.

CHAPTER 10

I was born in July in 1947 in Hamlet, North Carolina. I am 44 years old. My name is Byrum. We have a handicap sticker for the car, we can park in those places. My bad luck was brain damage. We had a car wreck.

I was asked to tell my story of my life into this tape machine because a girl who is my friend, that would be you, and takes me to movies and out to lunch that's what we do and she, I'm talking about you, said she'd pay me ten dollars for every tape I finished talking into. Is this how you want me to begin? You already know all this.

My father was okay and then when I got hurt he left you know street people they have these people they live under bridges, he did that. Every time I go to Charlotte I look for him but we don't know what he looks like so don't break your heart or waste your time he'll come home he knows where we live. One time he came to see me and took me to a Christmas parade. Don't be buying beer for him can I see your driver's license?

My mother was there when I woke up. I went to the mall and had to stay in the car. I was twenty years old then. My mother goes away sometimes.

A sad thing happened to me one time. A woman in a car. I cut my fingernails too short and they were bleeding and my mother cried. The lady and my mom rode in the car with me. I had suitcases. They are no Hardees back there only that bad food in the place except on some days.

I said don't leave me here. No one was in the room. Everybody but that man was crying and then I had to stay right where I was, don't move and don't go anywhere. I closed my eyes for a long time but the tears pushed out anyway. I remember that.

At six you have to get up at six because you can't just stay in bed all day. You're not lazy you can do it if you try. I never saw my own clothes because they put them somewhere and I had to wear these other people's clothes. Wash your own clothes do you think we are your slaves? I don't like rubber sheets. Do you want us to put the rubber sheets on the bed? Then get up.

I hit a woman and they put me in the chair and said don't move for the rest of the day. I was afraid of the big boys. One of them had a head on him so big it scared me. They called him a watermelon head. One of them had a blue face.

One time this girl vomited. She had to clean it up and that made her vomit again. Then we all vomited.

Sometimes when Sunday came that was another sad day. I would lie on the floor and wait for a visitor.

I had art class and finger painted. Everybody did that even the man with the blue face. Somebody ate the paint. Don't eat the paint.

The thunderstorms are bad. Captain Kangaroo said not to be afraid but he didn't lose power. The electricity went out and they had flashlights. Don't use up the batteries. Then it came back on but some people were gone they found them later. A man ate the collar off his shirt.

Okay, I'm up to now when I was about to come home and then the sad times stopped.

I was back home then. The government paid money you can get them to help you when you're eighteen but nobody told my momma until I was twenty and then I went back home. She cried. She said why didn't anyone tell me this?

I had a girl friend but I told you about that. She's gone. She told me I was handsome and I have nice clothes everyone says so, I spend my money on clothes and tapes and CDs and I give it to the girl friend. Don't give the girl friend money.

I came home and I was twenty and then I lived with my auntie. There were lots of people in the house which I did love that. My mom couldn't take it anymore.

I forgot to tell about Christmas. We could go home if people came to get us. I couldn't call anybody on the telephone. Thanksgiving was good. A man got scared when another man made a turkey sound when he bit into the turkey at the table and he ran away.

One time this girl, this is a sad thing again, this girl got a lot of presents and the next day they took them from her and put them in the basement. Don't go in the basement. She had too many presents and cake, too. Go to sleep. What do you think this is, a hotel?

I'm just trying to remember all of this because you said you wanted me to. I don't think about it much. Ricky told me you think too much.

We worked but not like in the chicken plant. We didn't get

paid. I had to count things. I never lost count. Count Count and Ernie. Sometimes there were bolts and washers. Six bolts, six washers, six nuts. You nuts count the nuts. You get credit at the snack bar. I bought drinks for people and Lance crackers and one time Krispy Kreme doughnuts we all had some because the people who owned the company sent a whole truck there. They were like eating clouds. They were like cotton candy but better. I bought a dozen and gave them to everyone at work last week. Wash your hands first.

The Lions Cub was nice to us. All the men brought us pizza. You could only eat two slices. No candy bars after four o'clock. I have asked about joining the Lions Cub here in Hamlet. They're going to let me know. I want to be a member. I hope they call me soon.

Is this enough about back then? I don't know how much to tell.

We had gym class. Don't look at the men's privates. I had a big boil on my hip and one on my back. I told him and he said I had to do the work anyway. It was so sore. I got punished. They always said you're a liar but I never was.

The tape is almost over on this side. I can see it.

I went to the bathroom just then. Now I got the other side on this tape player. This is harder than I thought it would be. But I want to do it. I came home when I was twenty and did a lot of good things and went to schools and worked in the workshop and then Mr. Russell gave me this job in the chicken plant and I have never missed a day in seven years. Mr. Russell is one of the nicest people I have ever known in my life.

This is what I do but you already know it. I clean up on the clean-up shift if Mr. Russell tells me to even if I already worked the day shift. He says I am their best worker. We put everything back where it's supposed to be. We get up the pieces of chicken that fell off the tables or belts. You can't stop to pick them up if you're working in the other shifts. Work fast. Time is money.

When I work in the daytime I sometimes stay at the fryer it's hot and when you skin the chicken breast it's easy to pull it off but if you drop it, just leave it there the clean up crew will get it. A big heavy woman slipped on some skin and the supervisor told her to be more careful. It took three of us to pick her up. I load the boxes when a truck comes in. I make a lot of money. Big money. The Price is Right. Big money big money.

They laughed at me on the fryer they said I passed gas it smelled so bad and I kept working and they kept talking about it and I said I didn't but it smelled bad I think someone else did but don't do that in public, go to the bathroom if you have to. It wasn't me. We can't go to the bathroom. I clean the men's and ladies' when I am on the night shift. You prop open the door with the mop bucket so they will know you're in there. If someone needs to use it you leave and close the door. One time the toilet didn't flush and people kept using it.

Mr. George Russell is the son of the big boss man, who is Mr. Charlie Russell who has a house here in Hamlet and one at the beach. He said I could come with him sometime and clean up that house if I wanted to and then swim in the beach. They are a very nice family. I love him like a father.

I turned off the machine because my Auntie just came in and read me a story in the newspaper that the man who invented Barbie dolls died a week ago. His name was Jack Ryan. I have lots of Barbie dolls and dresses and the Ken dolls, too, and clothes for them. I have the car and the beach chairs and sunglasses, they are hard to find. I collect them at the yard sales and flea markets. I got the first one I ever owned they saved it for me.

A man they called Tight Pants Tony almost got fired for stealing chicken nuggets and tenderloins. He took a bunch of boxes. They locked the doors so he can't steal that way. They fired him but he came back.

If you have to go to the bathroom you have to ask but they don't want you to. Tight Pants Tony had three demerits anyway. You get a half a demerit if you go to the bathroom too much. Then when you get three-and-a-half you get laid off. If you slip and fall down like that heavy-set lady, you get a demerit. If you fall down three times you get laid off. No cowboy boots or high heels. The woman had a piece of chicken in her hair. I told her and she pulled it out. When the supervisors aren't looking the mean women throw skin and cancer pieces at the young girls. That's where the one in the hair got from.

The gloves cost eight dollars. One woman melted hers when she got too close to the flame. It melted on her finger and then her finger looked like that man that had the blue face. Turn off the recorder when you stop talking.

I might get another job. I was thinking I could get me a job as bell boy. I have been wondering if I should ask anybody about it. There is nothing wrong with the nice people most of them anyway at the chicken plant but some people are mean and I stay away from them. Mr. Buck Ellis is always after me. That's life learn to live with it you will never find all good people until you die and go to heaven, but I thought maybe I could work as a bell boy.

I saw one in Raleigh last Christmas and I liked it. I could

stand there on the street ringing the bell and people would give me money to put in the bucket and I could give that money to people who needed it.

I know who dumped the grease out back in the pine trees. I saw him dump the grease and dumped the skin in the creek. Do your job and I'll do mine. That grease smells like hog manure I saw a hog killed one time he wouldn't die and they shot him the whole rifle empty, twelve bullets. That was a sad thing.

Last time I worked we were stepping on that gas line again. It's in the way. It sticks out under the fryer and we step on it. You get a demerit if you step on it. It's right where your feet go. Everybody says they have a hurt back but they say that's so we can collect disability. I already get it. Don't tell people about that, you have to learn not to put your foot in your mouth.

I have my flashlight. Lightning can't hurt you in a car and in a house but lightening balls can roll across the room and kill you. I saw the lightning balls one time in a house, they just floated toward me and then disappeared. I can call anytime, here's the number.

Wolves and bears don't live in Hamlet. You're safe here. People have been getting killed in Hamlet. They brought the casket to the institution and put Ronald in it. His head wouldn't fit in they told me about it.

I can wake up but the alarm clock might not go off. That little button is hard to find. It's hard to get my fingers on it and then I put it on the wrong dot one time. I wish you were here instead of the tape recorder. I will have this finished and give it to you Saturday. I can call. Call me anytime. Don't do it, stupid. Don't you know any better than to wake up people?

They made a movie right here in Hamlet, they had the Hollywood cameras and made the movie Billy Bathtub. It starred Justin Hoffman and our town which is very beautiful and an All American Town, looks like places used to look back in the old days. We had trains all day and night long.

It's been off but I turned it on because I fell asleep now it's four thirty I might cut it off and go to work early. It was a holiday yesterday and you couldn't work. I can wait outside if the doors are locked, don't touch them because the alarm might go off but there is no alarm it's just a sign. She said the alarms don't work nothing works.

God meant for chickens to die or he wouldn't have made fried chicken is what they told me so it's still sad sometimes, but you don't see the chicken head or eyes. In the hog, the eyes were crying and blood came out.

We get the parts, the breast and the thigh it's got a lot of meat on it and we get the strange pieces they make the fajitas out of that you just cut it up real little shreds, the machine shreds it and make them. It's Mexican food. We don't have many Mexicans in Hamlet but they got them in Siler City.

The machines break then what'll we do? If you put your finger in there they'll be eating your fingers instead of chicken fingers. I'm careful, but sometimes the men come up behind you and push you like you're going to fall into the machine, they're just kidding around. Some of the women hate the young women who come to work, Lois says they are jealous and full of meanness you don't know how mean most people are. Learn to live with it. Right? You go to college and are so smart.

I can go to work soon with all the lights on down there. They used to sell ice cream but now it's chicken. I could work in the ice cream plant but it's gone. MelloButtercup. The sign is on the ground out in the pine trees. I'm almost finished with the tape I can get ready for work. I'll put Barbie and Ken back in their house. I had them on my lap one on each leg. When you travel keep your wallet in your front pocket because of pickpockets.

I'll go to work early. I'll be the first one there.

Buck Ellis, Byrum's supervisor at the plant, had a face that looked like a slice of raw, cured ham. It was both pockmarked and grainy, like it had been salt-rubbed and hung up on his neck to age. His shoulders were the size of a boar hog's and his hands were thick and callused. He was fifty-seven years old and had lived in Richmond County his whole life.

"Now let me tell you something," he was saying to his nephew.

"I can't find my ear plugs," the boy said.

His nephew was 14 and had never hunted in his life.

"The boy hadn't never shot no bird," Buck had been telling his friends. "The boy hadn't never gone hunting," he had been exclaiming for weeks, saying it the same way someone else might remark that a person's never eaten a hamburger or never smiled or never had a drink of water.

"Don't you got any ear protectors, Buck?"

They were sitting in Buck's Silverado, which was stopped in the ruts in the dry, white, sandy road that ended at two trailers he had on the edge of what remained of the family land. Buck's brother, who ran a septic tank pumping service, also had his shop back there and had put up a sign on the highway that said, We're Number One with Your Number Two.

The trailers were past the shop and one was rented to a black woman who cleaned the Ellis house and worked at Capital Food Products. The other one, which had come loose while being towed down the road when it was new and wrecked and was then sold as salvage, was Buck's hunting lodge.

"When we get out there, don't shoot me, boy. You're going to get kind of aroused killing all those birds, but keep a eye out for where I am all the time."

"I know to be careful."

"You shoot someone and the next thing you know they got the gun legislation passed."

"I can't believe I forgot my hearing protectors."

"A man has a right to kill," Buck said.

"Yes sir, I know."

"You ever kill anybody, boy?"

"What're you talking about?"

"You need some trigger time. Every man's got to have some trigger time."

Buck dumped a package of salted peanuts into his mouth. He held the narrow cellophane container to his lips until it was empty and then tossed the wrapper out the window. The boy watched as a dribble of foam worked out his lips as he chewed. The more he chewed, the larger the mass in his mouth grew until Buck spun toward the window and spat the wad into the air.

"Bad," he said, still spitting pieces. "Gone bad. Rancid."

He took a long pull from the brown glass bottle in his hand and swished it around in his mouth before swallowing.

"Take a drink," he said and held the bourbon toward his nephew while at the same time taking a swig out of the Pepsi he had propped up in his crotch.

"Naw, I don't want any."

"You say you don't want any?"

It was Labor Day and bird hunting season began in earnest each year about this time. In less than an hour, more than a dozen of Buck's friends would be parked nearby, all of them spread out across the silage-cut cornfield waiting on the birds.

"Boy," Buck said and held the bottle pressing tightly against his nephew's chest while he, himself looked, not at the boy but out the windshield directly in front of him, as if he was so shocked he couldn't look at the young man. "Don't tell me that."

"What?"

"Around here, when a man offers you a drink," Buck said and paused and waited and then looked directly at his nephew, "you take it."

The bottle mashed so hard against his breastbone the boy put his hand on its neck and pulled it away just to relieve the pressure. He then accepted it from his uncle's hand and tilted it up to his lips. Within a couple of seconds, everything from his mouth to his eyes burned.

"That's how you do it," Buck said and took another drink himself, slowly reaching for the Pepsi and dragging it against his crotch just a little as he picked it up just for the feeling of it, just to make contact, just to give himself a manly sensation.

"Okay."

"Time to grow up, boy."

They had been practicing shooting for weeks. Buck had lent

him a shotgun which he took home and promptly had to return because his mother wouldn't allow it in the house.

"See that little gal over there," Buck said, pointing with the bourbon bottle toward the dark-skinned woman who had come out of her trailer with her hair on crooked and clothes that had either been slept in or been worn the entire past few days, the whole weekend, maybe. "You can have a little of that if you want."

"Well . . . ," he said, trying to find something else to follow it but coming up with nothing.

"You ain't scared of it, are you?"

"No, I'm not scared, it's just. . . ."

"It won't cost you nothing. She's part something else you know, Indian, Puerto Rican, Mexican or something."

"I mean. . . ."

"That's how she pays her rent," Buck said. "Works out just fine."

Jessie came right up to the truck on the driver's side and reached her hand in.

"You bring me one?" she asked.

"I might have," Buck said.

She was barefoot and a cat walked in and out of her legs and over her feet, stepping on them and trailing her tail across the woman's calves as she passed back and around and through.

"Give it to me," she said and reached past Buck and took the full bottle from the seat and walked back to her trailer, carrying the cat in her free arm.

"Let me tell you the joke about the gynecologist. You know what that is? Okay, this fellow was in bed with his wife and he nudged her and started with her and she stopped him and said, no, I can't, I got to see my gynecologist tomorrow. So he rolled on over and then a few minutes later, tried again, and she told him no, she had an appointment with the gynecologist. You following me, boy?"

"Yeah, I guess."

"So about fifteen minutes later, he nudged her again and said, well, I was just thinking, you ain't got a dentist appointment tomorrow, right?"

He laughed a long time and coughed and repeated the last line of the joke a few times and laughed some more and then took another swig from the bottle.

"You want to stop in on the way out and see that little gal over there?" he asked.

"I just, you know, I don't really care about it."

"Well, you'll be doing the waiting then, because old Buck gets the urge pretty bad when he goes hunting."

"Okay."

"Something about killing birds makes a man want to do it."

"When's everybody else getting here? Who all's it going to be?"

There was a cooler of beer covered with ice in the back of the truck and on top of the ice there were packs of luncheon meat sandwiches and a couple of boxes of Nabisco chocolate chip cookies. A few soft drinks were buried in the ice and the cooler, which was the size of a child's casket, had handles on each end to carry the weight.

"You want a sam-wich?" Buck asked.

"I'm not hungry right now," he said and then winced, remembering he might have been expected to say yes to every other offer, too. "Those crackers are still working on me," he added. "I ate three packs. I hope they weren't rancid."

"Eat half of this. You'll need it once we start."

Buck took a long swig of the bourbon and set it on the seat between himself and his nephew, leaning the neck toward the boy. He watched him out of the corner of his eye, laughing to himself as he saw the boy secretly look at the bottle and how it was leaning. Staring straight ahead again, like he had the first time he offered, he leaned the bottle just a half inch more toward his nephew.

"Drink your Pepsi, boy. I ain't going to bother you."

His nephew put his feet on the dash and retied his boots. He snorted up one nostril and then leaned toward the window and spit, and then, without realizing he was doing it, he pulled on his crotch, and set his own Pepsi down there, just like his uncle was teaching him.

It was September 2, 1991, in the Sandhills of North Carolina and for some people, in some places, very little had changed over the last half of the twentieth century. In the same way that contemporary CEOs were the masters of their universe, and knew it, Buck Ellis was the master of his, which was the universe bounded by life behind the stock of a shotgun, behind the wheel of a Chevrolet pickup, in his own home, and within the walls of a chicken plant in Hamlet where the men and boys who worked beneath him did what he said and feared him in some primal way.

A man out hunting with Buck Ellis knew there was a narrow line between killing birds and killing, by what would be seen as an accident, anyone who crossed him. The eerie sense of death that surrounded a tribe of men out hunting included, unspoken, the knowledge that you could be killed if you did not become a man in the way men who hunted, drank, and prevailed in their universe, became, were, and lived for.

The boy didn't know why he did what Buck told him to do, why he tried to become like Buck. He knew he had to. The men who worked for him in the chicken plant didn't know why they did what he said and crossed him very rarely, if ever. But they did what he said.

"Give me that bottle."

"Now you're talking," Buck said. "Talking like a man," he added and ruffled, gently and with true affection, his nephew's hair, who stretched his neck from one side to another, trying to get rid of the chills his uncle had caused to run up and down his spine. He swallowed his drink, took a swig of his Pepsi, and then unzipped his shotgun from its vinyl case. He pulled on the pump beneath the barrel and opened up the chamber, causing the gun to make the classic clicking and breaching sound so familiar to hunters, movie goers and watchers of violent television dramas.

"I like that sound," he said. "Don't you, Buck?"

CHAPTER 12

6 A.M.

Antonio Cotton was Carly's father. He and Lois had never married. He was also the great-grandnephew of Elizabeth Cotton, the famous singer and songwriter from the Depression era, who had written a ballad that had been covered hundreds of times called *Freight Train*, and he believed himself to be related to John Coltrane. He claimed the connection as did many other people in Hamlet and Dobbins Heights.

He was singing to himself now, Tuesday morning, 2½ hours before the fire would begin. He was going out for breakfast.

"Freight train, freight train, coming so fast, freight train, freight train . . ." he hummed some now, and then filled in the words when he felt like it, *"please don't say what train I'm on . . ."*

He lived alone in a room with a separate entrance that was in the house owned by his uncle and aunt, and that house was six streets away from where Lois and Carly lived. He had met Lois while visiting one day, nine years ago, when he was eighteen and Lois was twenty-three.

"Please don't say where . . ." he started, and then stopped as

scores from the night before came across the bottom of the television screen.

"No man have to marry me," Lois had said when she found out.

"But I will."

"You don't need to do me no favors," she said. "My momma raised us up by herself and I can do the same thing."

"But I will. I don't mind."

When Antonio had said 'he didn't mind,' he had thought it was a nice sentiment and showed his good will and generosity.

"You don't mind? I don't mind if I don't, then," Lois had told him. "I don't mind," she had muttered a few times, while walking off.

For years after that she addressed him as *I don't mind*, using it as his name, and she said it so much that whenever he heard the phrase used in casual conversation, he felt it.

He had given Lois a hundred dollars a month from then on. He saw Carly when Lois let him, and saw Lois every day for the past two years at work. He'd taken the job there when she'd mentioned that Mr. Russell was looking for a man to work in the cooler and freezer room, collecting the boxes and storing them and then getting them out when the trucks came, and to keep the flour bin filled.

Freight train, freight train, please don't tell what train I'm on . . .

He knew his daughter wanted to come to work today and stay until ten and he had cleared it with the supervisors just in case her mother actually let her. He cleaned his black-rimmed glasses at the sink in the bathroom, brushed his teeth and left the house to get breakfast at Hardees.

He drove a green 1987 Cadillac that was as clean inside and

out as one on the showroom floor. It was so much fun to drive he reflected on it in bad times almost like a heavenly destination, something like the way people dreamed of a vacation on a Polynesian Island, the way some people dreamed of cool air and shady days out of the broiling sun. It was comfort, seats like clouds, and smooth, the way life ought to be, smooth and quiet and dignified and easy, and generous, the way it felt to stop to let someone out of a parking spot in heavy traffic, to let a pedestrian cross, being in that Cadillac which was as green as wild mint, felt that good, was that refreshing, a vision, for Antonio, sometimes, of how life could have been had things gone better. Rich, as in love, as in blessed, as in divine, it felt that good to be in his car.

A church pamphlet lay on the leather passenger seat. Antonio was not only on the widows and orphans committee, like his father had been, but was one of the few men in the congregation who attended prayer services on Wednesday evenings. He liked his minister and the idea of ministering so much, he wondered why he didn't still, at his age, study to become one himself.

Two weeks earlier he and the minister had gone to supper together. They had driven into Rockingham and had eaten at the buffet line of the Golden Corral. He had spent part of the time talking to Reverend Bishers about Charlie Russell. After the discussion, Antonio had written, in an elegant hand, a letter to Russell and sent it anonymously, with no return address. He thought he might do something like this each month, something that would open the man's heart to God if it happened to arrive at just the right moment in his life, which, Antonio thought, judging from how stressed and unhealthy he looked, would be soon.

CHAPTER 13

It's still dark. Morning does seem to be coming slowlier today. You didn't tell me how much talking it would be. We can go out to the Sagebrush Saloon in Asheboro if you want to drive that far. Will your car make it?

I could be a cook. I learned everything you can cook with chickens. I learned all of it. My mom read me all the things you can make. I watch the cooking show. I watch it everyday. I could get a job in a restaurant and make this food. Can you get me a job like that? You can make chicken breasts in wine, stuffed chicken breasts, grilled chicken breasts with cucumber and pepper relish, chicken breast parmesan, sautéed chicken breast with clover and honey, chicken breast Santé Lucia, I like the sound of that one, baked chicken breast with cornbread and collards, Cajun chicken breast with sour cream and black bean sauce, and then the last one I remember is chicken breast with Italian saucers.

It's light. I'm walking now. I will be the first person there like I said before I have done that many times. I can take it. Be a man and learn to take it. If you can't go with the flow, get out of the kitchen. I don't know what I'll do this afternoon. Maybe I'll watch Gunsmoke and Sesame Street. Gunsmoke comes on first.

I guess I won't get married after all. I love children. Matt Dillon is tough but good. Miss Kitty owns the saloon. Festus rides a mule. A long time ago a man had a mule in town and it pulled a wagon and he went around and got junk and old boxes and newspapers and he was a nice man. Somebody told me he ate possums which I don't want to eat. I thought I might have a wife and children one day. I guess I won't.

Sometimes my legs get so tired. I have headaches but I can't stop to take the medicine until lunch time or break time but break time goes past and we forget about it. I keep all my quarters on my dresser and take eight with me each day. You put in two for a cracker and two for the drink and then I do that again in the afternoon when they let us take a break. Dimes are easy but you can't buy anything with them. I give them to children.

There's a dead deer behind the building beside the tracks. Some train hit it I guess. It'll smell bad soon, but lots of things around here smell bad. Deer don't have insurance. If you hit one you have to pay for the damage yourself. If you have a little car they go up the hood and into the windshield. Buck Ellis shot a deer with big antlers it looked like a moose. He had it in the back of his truck. He made me go outside and touch it.

I have my earphones with me. I can stop talking and play the radio part. Don't wear them inside the building you might not hear something coming and get hurt. The little forklift is quiet. They picked me up one time in a box up to the ceiling. Why were you in the box? Is what people asked me. I was hiding from the man who told them where I was. He likes to put wrapping tape on me. He's just kidding around.

You can't give blood to a turnip. Lots of people play jokes, it's just human nature. I don't have to do anything unless somebody asks me to.

CHAPTER 14

Louise, Ellie's mom and great-granddaughter of Emily, worked in an adult day care where she was the social director. It was a good job for her. The pay was better than chickens, better than ice cream, and she got health insurance. She made the old folks laugh and she had known most of them for years, before they started going to the center, so she had plenty to talk about.

"I found something," she had told Ellie a few weeks ago. "I was in the attic and I found pages of this diary. I knew about it from before but then I forgot where it was. It's been years since I'd seen it. I've been reading it. Now I want you to have it."

Ellie had taken it to her room when she got it. The binding was broken and silverfish were between some of the pages, but the ink was dark and the words were clear.

"I love this," she had told her mother later that night. "It's so interesting. I wish I'd known these people. I wish I could time travel."

The diary was part of the treasure of old clothes and letters and photographs that Ellie and her mother had been unearthing for weeks.

"It's the best find yet."

This morning, Ellie was up as early as her mom and told her she was going to work at the chicken plant for a few weeks. They had a box of Bear Claw pastries from the Food Lion bakery, and they were eating them and drinking coffee when Ellie found the right moment to say it.

"Surely you're kidding?"

"No. It'll be a lark. I just need to pick up some extra money. Don't worry about it."

"You're doing this for Byrum, right?"

"Well, that could be."

"Could be? It's not the money, is it? I thought you were okay that way. I wish you hadn't quit the job at JoJo's."

JoJo's had been a shop in Rockingham that sold funky clothes, mostly second-hand.

"Well, Mom, number one they went out of business . . ."

"Oh, yeah."

"And number two, my old car wasn't going to make the drive there and back much longer."

"I know."

"Besides, I thought I had enough saved for awhile, but I was wrong."

"You can't fix Byrum's life. What does Ricky have to say about it?"

"I don't know. Whatever. It's just for a little while."

"The chicken plant? This is very awful and very weird, either way it's not a good idea."

"Gwen and me will laugh and make a big adventure out of it. We got it all planned out. Not to worry, Mom."

Ellie drove four blocks and let off the gas and let the old Tercel coast. The wheels revolved silently, then they stopped. The little silver hubcaps with the Toyota trademark stopped upside down on all four wheels, and a fine mist of green coolant sprayed from a crack in a hose.

Like the Overland that had broken down on the road when the trains were about to meet head on and where the townspeople were rushing to stop the collision, Ellie's car rolled against the curb in front of one of the many turn-of-the-century houses from the glory days of the merchant class. This was another Queen Anne, with turrets and gables and sloping, auxiliary rooflines. It had gables meeting the main roof with overhangs that touched the shingles like upswept balletic arms, as if the dormers had floated onto the main roof and landed in an *umpriea'* of grace and repose.

She took the diary off the seat. The script looked as if it had been applied to the page with the point of a knife, as if each fraction of each letter had been carved as a work of art like calligraphy, as if each letter, each word was its own story, written, she thought, so slowly it would have driven her insane, would have put her into the asylum to have been forced to repeat it. What kind of woman would have had the patience to do this and what kind of patience would it be?

The kind of woman, she understood from reading some of the diary already, who was prepared by hours and days and years of being still, of learning to self-suffocate, of learning to express her cravings and bursting energies by merely blinking her eyes.

(diary): I am a bottle of nerve tonic. The weeks pass like vacant, dry Sundays. Like days that never end. I ran out of the house. She ran out of the house. They brought her back. I brought me back.

I remember being sickened to realize I was still alive. That happens a lot. Actually that's true. Then Milly does something and I'm glad I'm here.

Sometimes I disappear in a swoon. He can have me then. I think he did. I wasn't sure until recently.

My vision clears sometimes and I am marching. I am once again the insurgency of impulse and of chaos and whim. I remember going up to a row of shabby houses where there were barrels of meat all along one side, and even the heads of slaughtered animals, and dogs, lots of dogs pulling pieces of bone and tissue. It wasn't houses but behind the butcher shops of Elgin Street, and I don't remember how I got there except it was when I'd been out walking and thought to myself, why do I have to know exactly where I'm going?

He'd asked me where I was going and I said something and then later I thought about it and wondered why a person has to know every minute of the day where she is going, what she is doing. That's when I walked straight along until I came to the houses and the shops.

Later.

I drank a cup of very black and very bitter tea. There are things you can drink that fix the problem. I don't know what they are. They say they are not safe.

Later.

There are blue, satin curtains and gold angels in the room. There is furniture that Mattie polishes every single day. She doesn't have to. I never told her she had to polish the bare arms of every chair every single day. I never said she had to remove every item from the tops of every surface and polish. My arguments run out of me and bump into everything in the room. They can't get anywhere. They can't get out. My words are absorbed by the fabrics and broken up by the heavy legs of tables and the massive, masculine bulks.

Ellie heard a noise and saw a woman in a robe scuffling with an aluminum storm door that had closed against her when she bent over to pick up a newspaper. A man leaned out and pushed the door away so she could stand. A child's head appeared between them, as if she had stuck it through a hole in a painted backdrop at the fair, just the face for a moment until she wriggled past her parents and sprinted into the yard with a miniature black Schnauzer at her heels. Someone going past blew a horn and the family looked up and waved.

(diary): The chairs are slippery. Sitting in the dining room on the chairs at the table is an act of balance. I have to brace my feet on the floor and keep myself pushed into them.

The light is refracted by the beveled glass along the top of the windows and it makes him look like two or three of him. Milly loves to be alive. It's truly not as if she's trying to make up for Caroline, for me. She is a daughter of the South, of my own South. I don't want her to grow up. I don't want to have any more children. He can take me when I don't know it. Though he is nice about it. So that's what he did.

I have been discouraged from writing. Miss Wharton was also discouraged. Yet, she did it and they don't mind if I read it. If it's perfectly normal and decent to read it, then why is it not to write it? Sometimes words are such an undercurrent of my days I feel I am talking to myself, talking out loud, that they're slipping out. I murmur in my dreams. I hear myself. There is no one else there to listen. Well, he does come in to say goodnight. He did stay that one time. I can write all the letters I want. I can keep the diary. All of that is in the rules.

I wear slacks and run.

Later.

I can make myself the object of sentimental pity. It's easy. I can do it. I will never ask my delightful daughter to avert her thoughts. What a messy trap. I am a frugal habit of restraint. I was. I am excess now. I am a dog on the street. I am the entrails I stepped over. I am red-faced and wet and livid with delightful torment.

Later.

I can't have any more children. I don't want to. Spring bonnets and Greek art, what do I care? The boy next door has the dimple that Caroline once had. There's a book out called *The Fall of Man*. I laughed so hard when I saw it. He asked what was so funny. I laughed until I sounded like I had the croup. He laughed, too. He enjoys me. He doesn't know. I keep thinking of Euripides and want to sing a song about you rip a dees you rip a does, and dress up like a plantation house slave and put on black face and join the minstrel show. I want to get away.

Later.

I'll have this child.

Later.

I won't.

I am her, Ellie began to think, still not driving. If I am anyone, then I must be her. She is the 'I am', and the 'I am not', of me. Her daughter was the last of the ladies, of the grand ladies. Then the daughter of that daughter, she thought, was Grandma Anita, and she worked in the ice cream plant. Now I am on my way there. Now I am what we have come to, what we have become. But, she thought, I am what we were, as well. I am what she was. I am the excess and the regret. I am that.

She drove slowly. She began to think in the cadence of the diary: *I am the this and the that.* Her radio was off. *I am the right and the wrong.* It was so early. *I am the decent and the indecent. The good and the bad.* There was so much to do, that had to be done, and so much in the way. *I am this day. I am the day that must be lived. I am the girl that was. I am him and me.*

I am the child and the mother and the daughter. I am all of them.

CHAPTER 15

6:30 A.M.

Charlie Russell had three children who worked with him in the business, which had a plant in Georgia and failing acquisitions in other states. He was in his late sixties. He did not dress like the executive in charge of a business that employed hundreds of people in three different states. He wore open-collar shirts and wrinkled, casual slacks.

Lately, he looked like a human variety of a chicken biscuit, his face doughy and puffy, mottled white as biscuit flour, his eyes reddish and fried, his lips pale brown and rolled like crust.

Kindness to his workers, he had discovered, was repaid by laziness and dishonesty and an atmosphere that turned the entire job site into recess or lunchtime at a junior high school. The workers were unable to grow up. The harder they were asked to work, the more devious they became.

They played the slow down game.

They played the not me game.

They played the I didn't see nothing game.

Charlie had recently tried acquisition as a way to gain a vertical integration of his products. This had gone badly, and the debt and failure had changed him. Debt had made him crazy. Debt had made him hateful.

It had made him remote and distracted.

"You won't talk to me," his wife, who was sixty-six, a year younger than Charlie, said. She'd married him 48 years ago, when she'd been 18. He'd been on the receiving end of this same conversation countless times.

Dear Dr. Atkins,

I own a food processing business. I read one of your books. If you will do me the honor of reading this letter and possibly meeting with me, at your convenience, I think we could do business together.

"I call you, you never call me. I talk like a dodo bird trying to keep the conversation moving, and you grunt," she said.

I believe in the high protein, low carbohydrate diet you have discovered. As we know, chicken is healthier for you than beef or other high-fat foods.

"I grunt?" he asked her. He was at the desk in his bedroom. He wore size XXL boxer shorts and the same in a V-necked tee shirt. He was fifty- or sixty-pounds overweight, like many men his age who gained of a couple of pounds a year once into their thirties. He cradled the phone between his shoulder and his ear.

"What are you doing? Your voice is far away. I hear paper," she asked.

I could supply you with whatever chicken pieces, styles, cooking variation and weights and flavors you might want in what I would propose, loosely, to call the Atkins Capital Food Selections.

"You hear paper? I didn't know paper could talk. What's it saying?"

"George sounds as bad as you," she said. "What's going on? Is the company in trouble?"

I see a market in the recipes and design, something like the Lean Cuisine. Green is a good color on boxes. But we would have the pros work on that. What I am offering are the services and expertise of our entire business as well as the connections we have with the prepared and fast food market. The potential to get this into one of the big chains is real and hardcore.

"Just the usual trouble. I'm trying to work on something here. Are you coming up?"

"I thought you were coming home. Today, even. You said after Labor Day. After your golf. How can you play with your fingers aching like they do?"

He struck out the word hardcore.

We have a loyal workforce. Some of them are seriously over-weight, and I can see using them as focus groups for the product, without any added cost. They could even be sent home with the product for testing. They would be open to this, as they like to take the product home with them already.

"Come up here. Things are too busy to leave now."

He held his hand in the air and flexed his fingers. Pain shot all the way to his elbow where it concentrated on where the piece of shrapnel the size of a chicken's eye was embedded. After the pain localized it did what it always did, which was to ride back down his arm and lodge in his finger joints so that to move them felt like his bones were sticking through his skin.

"You don't want me to. You don't care. You don't want me to come visit."

"I care," he said. He had told her a hundred thousand times that he cared for her. "I'm just busy."

"Other men retire."

"Well, that's not likely."

He had thought of himself as the patriarch of a loose clan of people who came to him for help, for jobs, for need, and, if they did right, he gave them those things. Like any good father, if they did wrong, they were punished.

On the big-screen television set, a year-old golf game was being re-televised. Hale Irwin lined up a putt. He squatted down, he sought to understand the route the ball would take, he walked to one side of it and to the hole and then back again, and then he lined himself up and tapped the ball from 57 feet, the graphics on the screen said. The ball went north and then began to come down, swinging in a slow arc as if Irwin had intentionally hit it way off and then had a magnet in the hole that pulled it back. The ball rode over the undulations and even went around the back of the hole before actually reversing itself and dropping in.

"Damn," Charlie said.

"What?"

"Hale Irwin," Charlie said.

"You're watching TV and writing something on paper while you're talking to me? Is that it?"

Later, he opened a package of Pepperidge Farm chocolate chip cookies and ate until they were gone. He took the empty bag and puffed it open. It was lined with silver foil. He put his hand in it and pulled it up to his wrist. He held it against his chest, as if he had an injury and his arm was in a sling, the bag the cast around his hand.

"Oh, my hand. Medic! Medic!" he called, still living four decades of wartime souvenir pain.

Everyone in his generation remembered hearing about President Hoover's promise of a 'chicken in every pot' and who anywhere on this earth would have imagined that idea had transformed into a chicken restaurant on practically every block.

The intermittent hand pain which came on without warning was his only physical souvenir. He had returned from Europe not in a plane, but on a rolling, seasick, crowded Liberty Ship which he and his friends had held together with prayers, they told each other, so flimsy and thin it had seemed, spot welds popping as it creaked and twisted. In the middle of the Atlantic, he'd tossed all his gear over the side, his rotted sleeping bag, his socks, his helmet and liner, even his leather flying jacket and flight pants, which would have now been worth something. He never wanted to see anything associated with the war again.

Images and sounds superimposed on his daily activity. They started on their own and ended on their own, and he often had to talk over them, think around them, shake them out of his mind. He knew from newspaper accounts and documentaries made decades after the war that many people had this same mental activity.

His fingers relaxed and the pain receded and he reached for the kettle to start water for coffee but forget he had the Pepperidge Farm bag on his hand. He knocked the pot off the stove onto the floor. Cool water spread out on his bare feet. He shook the package off and let it drop onto the kitchen table.

He gathered up a pile of mail and flipped through it, leaving most of it unopened except for a large envelope that was the size and firmness of a big, printed, wedding announcement. His name was written ornately but there was no return address, though the postmark was Rockingham. Inside, on the heavy stock, was a letter. It read:

My dear friend,

How are you? I just had to send a note to tell you how much I love you and care about you.

I saw you at your job. I see you everyday, in fact, at work. I waited all day, hoping you would notice. As evening drew near, I gave you sunset to close your day and a cool breeze to rest you, and I waited. You never showed up. Oh yes, it hurts, but I still love you.

I saw you fall asleep the other night and longed to touch you, so I spilled moonlight upon your pillow and face. Again I waited, wanting to rush down to you, so we could talk. Please talk to me. I have many gifts for you. You awakened and rushed to work. My tears were in the rain.

Oh, if you would only listen to me. I love you. I try to tell you in the blue sky and quiet, green grass and the music that is all around you. If you would only let me walk with you and talk with you. We could, some day, spend an eternity together.

I know how hard your life is. I really know! I want to help you. I want you to meet my father. He wants to help you. My father loves you, too. I know you are suffering. I know you do not mean to be as you are now. I understand you do not want to be mean to everyone.

Just call Me. Please do. I can help you. You are free to choose Me. I know that. I made it that way. I have chosen you because I love you and I know you need Me. I will wait for you.

Your friend,
Jesus.

CHAPTER 16

A half hour before her shift began at Capital Foods, and two hours before the fire, Martha drove her two sons to get breakfast and then on to day care and kindergarten. She had supervised the fryer line the past week and was sick of the heat and the smell and hoped she would be somewhere near the freezer or cooler.

The high point of her day was getting home and taking off her grease saturated clothes and locking the door to the bathroom and easing down into a long bath with no noise and no children. She loved it so much she even paid for the extra hour to keep her kids at the day care, where the five-year-old joined the four-year-old after school. She came for them after she cleaned up and felt human, or, as she once told her husband Eldon, "not human, because that's what we are and look at us," but something, she said, she wasn't when she came home from work.

Her husband worked in live-haul for Perdue Poultry. He was often asleep while she was at work. Chickens in commercial broiler/fryer houses were uncaged, ran free, or more accurately, walked since they were limited in the amount of space to move around. They were caught at night using red light which kept them calm. Live-haul catchers and drivers made more than processing plant workers.

"He's trying to hit me," the four-year-old said.

"Don't hit your brother."

The biggest house where Eldon caught fryers was five hundred feet long, and this particular farm had three of them. Five hundred feet was almost the length of two football fields end-to-end. They were so big Eldon felt like he'd played two continuous games of the sport when he'd finished. Tired and beat up, cut by claws and beaks, filthy and red-eyed from the ammonia fumes.

The houses raised 15,000 to 20,000 birds every five weeks or so, depending on feed conversion. Dust, feathers and the smell of ammonia were a part of Eldon's skin and hair so that on a particularly busy and fatiguing night, when he came home in the early morning, too tired to have even slipped out of his coveralls, he looked a bit like he'd been, not tarred, but dusted and feathered. Even when he drove the Roanoke Chicken Hustler, with either the fan on it or the forks for lifting the cages, he was covered with the debris. His children called him Frankenchicken, and sometimes he chased them with his hands out in front like the conventional monster in pursuit.

"He's going to touch my leg," the four-year-old said.

"Don't touch his leg," she said.

The boys were strapped in with the seat belts but the five-year-old was moving his hand along the seat toward his brother. He inched it so slowly only his brother would have been aware of the progress, but the part of the torture that was most fun was the time it would take before it would make contact.

"He's getting closer. Mom."

"If you touch him I'll bust you one good."

Neither Eldon or Martha had finished high school, having hated the school experience worse than anything. "I'd rather take a beating than to have ever gone back to school," Eldon had often said. "Me, too," Martha had said at the time. School had felt not only confining and suffocating, but had seemed merely something that was keeping them from getting on with life.

"He's touching my pants."

The boy stopped short of contacting the material and moved his finger closer and then away, closer and then away, all the while forcing his brother against the door panel.

"I'm going to slap both of you, that's what I'm going to do."

Even though Martha and Eldon regretted their decisions at times, they never admitted it to anyone, not even each other. They quit school and married and had their children and bought their mobile home and they could drink and cuss and screw and watch television and raise their boys and no one, not teachers or parents, could tell them anything, except at work.

"I want a sausage, egg and cheese."

"We'll get what's on sale," Martha said. "Whatever they have on special is what you're getting." They pulled in to Hardees, which had a sign with pale red letters on a blue background. Under that sign was a white marquee that held the messages announcing the deals. This day, for breakfast, there was the two for $2 BEC, and for supper the eight-piece, four-biscuit fried chicken meal for $5.99.

Both boys, who could barely read, already knew how to interpret whatever letters were on the marquee. They understood all the combinations there could be with the letters for steak, sausage, bacon, chicken, cheese and egg. They could figure the

SEC, the STE, which had a different meaning for the S than the SEC, they knew the CB and the BE.

"I don't want the bacon egg and cheese."

"I don't either."

The drive-through was long. She parked. She took one boy in each hand and walked them into the building. She saw Antonio at the back of what seemed to be the fastest moving line and got behind him.

"Good morning," he said. "How're you today?"

"We're all right," she said. "These boys are killing me, but we're making it."

"What kind of trouble are you giving your mom?"

"No kind."

"We're not doing anything."

"They don't want the special."

"I want something different."

"The bacon falls off. I want the sausage."

"Bacon? Who said it's got bacon on it?" Antonio asked.

"That's what it is."

"That 'B' doesn't stand for bacon."

Antonio could see both boys going through a list, in their minds, of what else it could be.

"What is it, then?"

"That's a booger egg and cheese biscuit," Antonio said.

"You're lying."

"No, he's not," Martha said. "And you're going to eat it. Every dad-gummed booger of it."

"I'm not eating that. He is, though," he said and pointed to his younger brother who got mixed up in what was reality and what wasn't, knowing that somehow his older brother might actually make him eat boogers, that somehow, even though his rational thinking knew there wasn't such a biscuit, that he might, sitting in the blue plastic booth, unwrap the biscuit and find it full of boogers sprinkled on top of the cheese like black olive pieces on a pizza.

"I am not eating it," he said.

"You're eating it," his mother said. "Or starve."

Tears peeked out of the duct on the inside corner of his eyes and in much less than a second, his brother had seen them.

"He's crying, the baby."

"We're just teasing with you," Antonio said. "I'm sorry I played that joke. There're no boogers."

"No boogers, just snot. Snot egg and cheese, that's what SEC stands for."

Martha ordered one double special for the boys and one for herself. She was hungry. She was ready to drop her sons off at their schools and get on to work and on with her life wherever it was going. She chomped into the biscuits so hard and so fast she bit her own finger where she'd been holding the top half of the biscuit.

"Now look what you made me do," she said to her sons.

Antonio worked with her and spoke to her everyday, but he had gone over to the African American side of Hardees to eat. He knew not to sit with them, just as Martha, fond of him as she was, knew not to ask him to. There were no signs making anyone do anything, but in fast food places all over the South, the blacks had a side where they congregated each day and the whites another.

Antonio ate slowly. He missed his daughter, but knew she was coming to work that day with her mother. It had all been arranged.

CHAPTER 17

6:45 A.M.

When Charlie Russell was in the Eighth Air Force and flying the missions over Germany, he was nineteen years old, just married, and had learned by letter he'd had his first child, a son. In a specific kind of happiness and hope for the future, he named his son George Bonny Russell.

George Bonny was up early Tuesday morning working on a report that dealt with everything from their own problems with theft and dishonesty and poor workmanship, to live broilers, which they received already deceased, to the product out his own door.

Running two shifts meant they, in Hamlet alone, processed 60,000 pounds of chicken parts and shredded packets a day. Each worker had to handle, cut up, fry, freeze or pack at least 600 pounds of chicken each day. Given that a chicken breast yielded less than a half-pound of meat, each worker doing that job had to process at least 1,200 breasts a day, or, with lighter weight birds, even more.

"Is everyone up?" George called as he heard his family moving around.

At 7½ actual hours of work, the cutters and pullers handled 160 breasts an hour, or about three a minute, or one every twenty seconds, which they did while talking nonstop and laughing and paying little attention to their work, simply on automatic and skilled by the repetition of it all.

They were also skilled and even casual in their thieving and so unrepentant they would even stick a couple of frozen chicken breasts or a handful of frozen strips into their pockets at the end of the day, and how could he catch that? It was one thing to catch someone with sixty pounds in a box, another thing to frisk everyone going out the door. The full boxes, though, were what hurt them.

He lost two boxes a day. $490 per day. $2,940 per week. $149,940 a year.

That was more than his entire income. It was surely more than his father made because at this point in the business his father took no salary at all while trying to come out from under the debt. He lived on what he'd saved and invested.

"Who's crying?" George called to his wife, hoping that the child-crisis did not require his intervention.

That amount of money was equal to more than seven supervisors' wages, more supervisors than they had on any one shift. He could not let any of them go. It was possible he could do without one or two, but not all of them. If he let the one or two go, and asked more of the remaining, he'd have to offer them more and take on extra duties, himself.

"Can you get whoever that is to stop?" he called.

The whole chicken industry was an odd duck, he thought. It started out a woman's job, woman's work on the farm, and now it was again, in some ways, only they didn't own what was there, just did the work on the lines.

"We're settling down. Take it easy," he heard his wife say.

In the nineteenth century, it was thought that only women had the right amount of patience and gentleness to raise poultry, George read from a report in front of him, which went on to compare that concept to one of his heroes, Frank Perdue, who made the ad that said "it took a tough man to make a tender chicken."

"Be glad you're not raising chickens back in the late 19th century," he said to his wife.

Broilers, long ago, that were killed for meat, were simply old laying hens that ran free outside and then slept in little chicken houses at night that became, over the years, bigger and bigger until the chickens were never let out. These modern houses were owned by the farmers who owned the land and tended the chickens, but the birds and the feed and all the decisions were the property of the big slaughter companies like Gold Kist, Townsend and Perdue. The farmers were paid on a formula of how much feed they used in how long a time to produce a given sized bird.

The chickens were caught by hand by a live haul crew like Eldon's, loaded into coops and shipped on big open trucks, twelve birds to the coop, to the slaughter house. Until that moment, the chickens had had two square feet each to live, "running" loose on the sawdust- and woodchip-covered ground inside the house. Once caught, they were squeezed together like clothes in a suitcase, packed and pushed and fitted until there was no way to move.

"Honey, I'm going to be late today," George called to his wife as she was leaving the room. "I just got to finish up this reading and make something out of it. I got to figure out where we belong."

Once loaded on the trucks, the birds were on their way to be hung on shackles or hooks, stunned electrically, bled, defeathered, eviscerated, inspected, chilled, graded, packaged and shipped to places like grocery stores or Capital Foods.

"Aren't you finished yet?" she asked.

The problems, as George saw them, that affected the quality of the meat started with bruising, and the breast was the most bruised part, followed by the wings and legs. According to his research, 42% of live haul birds ended up with bruised breasts. This was not counting the DOA at the plant. Like people, fatigue from traveling made them less agitated once at the slaughter house. A long trip on the truck was good, except the stress, scientists' had discovered, associated with hauling them slowed their digestive tract clearance—they ended up with more feces inside their bodies—and increased what they called the 'live shrink' which had nothing to do with psychiatrists but involved live weight loss.

Birds needed lots of air, and the longer they sat stuffed into the coops on the trucks, the hotter they got and the more contamination of the carcass occurred. Even though growers stopped feeding the chickens 12 hours before they were caught, the gastrointestinal tract was not empty.

"Did you boys use the bathroom yet?" George heard his wife yell to their three sons.

Longer than 12 hours without food caused the birds to lose the mucus linings in their intestines and when that happened, fecal material in the bottoms of the shipping cages had a reddish-orange color and made the intestines so weak they broke open easier during evisceration.

"You sit on the commode and try. You hear me," his wife said, and he knew she was talking to their youngest.

Being careful, he read, during the loading and unloading caused less broken legs and broken wings, the increase of which, however, did benefit Capital Foods because they could use all the broken parts and reform the meat into patties and nuggets.

The use of blue or red lights was effective on chickens and in the live haul and slaughter part of the plant for calming the broilers. Bright lights got them agitated, so lighting was kept low. The birds, once hung up, had to be stunned. They were electrocuted for two to eleven seconds. Like people, it took more to kill some birds than others. When the amps got too high, which happened when supervisors wanted to speed up the line or when someone set the current improperly, the result was wing hemorrhages, red skin, poor feather removal, broken bones from thrashing about and blood splashes in the meat.

"And wipe yourself like I showed you," his wife yelled.

One of the big problems for the slaughter houses was to minimize the number of birds improperly bled and to reduce the number that had not yet died before they entered the scalder. The way the bird's head was positioned during slaughter was critical for bleeding and all that related to how they were shackled into the head and toe-bar guides. In other words, if the bird didn't cooperate and hold his head just right, the slice slipped.

If the head was out of position, the trachea and esophagus would be severed instead of slit and that made it difficult to remove the head and lungs, which also ended up giving a benefit to Capital Foods because they got all the damaged parts that couldn't be sold in a grocery store, and got them at a cheap price.

The birds were scalded by immersion for 1 1/2 to 3 1/2 minutes, which helped in feather removal. If the bird was alive when it entered the scald tank, George wrote in his notes, the trachea, esophagus, lungs, crop, gizzard and air sacs became contaminated with scald water. This made a red carcass and collapsed lungs, very difficult to remove. They received many red-carcass birds.

After the scalder, the carcasses went to the feather-plucking machines, which also caused broken wings especially if the rubber fingers were worn or out of position. Fecal contamination was possible during evisceration if the vent opener and draw hand were misaligned or the intestines, as George had noted before, were weak.

Contaminated carcasses had to be washed, trimmed or vacuumed at a reprocessing station, which was expensive, and held up getting to the chilling and packaging area, where rapid chilling down to forty degrees limited the pathogenic bacteria and increased shelf life, especially when a good amount of chlorine was used in the chiller water. After the chill water the carcasses were hung on drip line for a couple of minutes.

Wing damage, George read, was caused by wings caught in the coop door, human hanger workers acting too rough with the birds once in the slaughter house, the toe guards out of line, the pickers not adjusted and trouble with the catchers like Eldon in the houses, which produced what were called field bruises or breaks. Generalized carcass bruising could be caused by stunning voltage too high, as well as too much density in the grow-out houses, no place to stand, no place to sit, no way to get from one place to another.

"Well, honey, you've got an upset stomach. I didn't know. You can stay home today," he heard his wife say to their son.

Oily birds were a problem with nutritional imbalance, or a high scald temperature. Off-odors were a shipping and processing temperature problem, and all the problems, George noted, either allowed his company to have cheaper access to the meat, or caused his own quality control problems.

Abstract 157: Effects of raw cottonseed meal on carcass characteristics. Gossypium.

"I'll need to eat in a few minutes," he told his wife. "Unless I stay home. I got too much on my mind to go to work, if that makes any sense. Of course I'm going. Just dreaming."

CHAPTER 18

6:50 A.M.

I'm at work. My watch is blinking I never can stop it once it starts I can get another one at Wal-Mart, they are $6.95 plus tax, give a ten dollar bill for that.

The building is locked. There's a man asleep around back. He's sitting in a truck that got unloaded this morning. The men that unloaded it must have left already because no one's here. I guess he's sleeping because he's waiting to get loaded back up with something. He's in the cab. The trailer's backed up to where they do the loading. It's dark in those empty trailers. I get scared when I go in they might drive off. Somebody might play a trick on me. Then what would I do?

They locked me in the freezer one time. Lois let me out. I don't want to get hurt. I pretended like I was laughing when they let me out. You told me I could tell people when I was scared but I can't. They make fun of you and you never hear the end of it. You don't understand the people I work with or else you wouldn't say that. You're just a nice girl.

The cars are going by I wave to them so they won't think I

am trying to do something wrong like rob or break the windows beside the door. I couldn't break them I don't think, they are thick glass you can't see out they look like bricks stacked on top of each other and beside each other with mortar in between, my father laid brick until he stopped I helped him once I think, they told me I did.

There are only two windows in the whole building you can never see if it's raining one time it snowed and the supervisors played a joke and nobody told us until we went out at the end of the day. It was like the whole world had changed and everything was beautiful and cold and the air was good not like the bad air inside the building and I knew that God had made it snow to make us all happy.

I love my job but the chicken gets so greasy and the floor is greasy and you can't slip and fall and the vat is bubbling and the little sparks of grease pop sometimes and you get little spots all over the apron and in your face and then you go outside and it's all white and beautiful. I wish I had not been in that wreck. I will never be a normal person.

I have a lot of jokes I've been thinking up and people tell them to me and I remember them and I have a bunch ready to tell to people. One is about Superman who was Clark Kent, and it's what is Superchicken's real name. Cluck Kent. What is a rooster who wakes you up? A alarm cluck. Why do baby chickens talk all the time because talk is cheep. What day do chickens hate most of all? Fry-day. Why is a chicken skeleton afraid because he has no guts. I know lots of the jokes. What did the chicken do when he saw a bucket of fried chicken he kicked the bucket. What happened when the chicken was born with feathers pointing the wrong way she was tickled to death.

We get chickens in here that are all messed up the parts look funny. Kentucky Fried Chicken is the best tasting of all you we don't make anything for them but we do for the grocery stores we make the chicken tenders and nuggets and the breasts patties that's mostly pieces that go into the forming machine and come out looking like a patty.

I been turning the tape off and on I don't have enough to say to fill it up anymore. It's light outside now and there are more people driving down the road and a woman I can't see who has parked her car I think it's you across the street what are you doing here maybe it's not you.

I'm not married and I guess I never will be. You told me not to think it, that there was someone for everyone. The main thing is not to think about things that make me sad there are better things to do with life than be sad. You say that. Women can cook very well. My mom and my auntie can cook about anything. I forgot to make up my bed. My cousin is always in trouble. Here comes Mr. Ellis I always feel like he's going to hurt me. Maybe he didn't see me.

I keep talking in here like you told me. You said just turn it on and walk around with it and keep talking telling what I'm thinking and seeing. That's what I'm doing now and you can hear the traffic and the horns just then. I like to watch the movies with you and eat lunch especially at either Golden Corral or Sagebrush Saloon. I love the peanuts there. Thank you for taking me to those places.

"I wasn't saying anything Mr. Ellis. I'm making a tape recording I'm turning it off now."

"Come here, boy."

"Do you hear the one about chickens playing basketball, Mr. Ellis?"

"What about it?"

"They kept fowling out."

"You ever shot a rifle, Byrum?"

"No sir, I don't want to do that."

"See them guns in that rack in the truck?"

"Yes sir."

"Me and that boy killed 18 doves yesterday."

"18?"

"Come over here with me," Buck said.

"I got to get ready to go inside."

"Come over here," he said and took him by the arm. "Leave that tape recorder there. You don't got to listen to rock music all day long."

"No sir."

"Hold this shotgun. Feel it. Heavy, isn't it?"

"Yes sir. It's heavy. I hope it doesn't go off."

"Feel that barrel."

"Yes sir."

"Gun oil."

"Gun oil."

"Now aim it there at those trees and squeeze off a round."

"It'll be loud."

"Yeah, it'll be loud. Don't point that thing at me, Dumbo. Aim it that way."

"I got to go inside."

Byrum put his hands over the back of his head and ran away.

"I'm going to shoot you, boy."

He heard him yell and cock the gun and then laugh. He scooted inside the entry door that was beside the two glass brick windows. Other men laughed along with Buck.

"Mr. Ellis was trying to scare me," he said once inside.

"Don't you pay any attention to him," a woman said. "He's just a mean, old redneck piece of trash."

"I ran. So fast."

"You're safe now, Byrum. You're safe in here."

PART III

The Tao of Chickens, or The Many Ways to Die

Ellie remembered the flat-roofed brick structure, which Gwen had described as drab as a crab. There was a smaller building on the opposite side of the road. It was a model of the larger building with the same red clay brick and same proportions.

Soon after she parked, other people got out of their cars and walked to the building, putting on their aprons or smocks and hairnets as they nodded to each other or continued on in silence.

I am not this or that. Not yet. I can see what to do now. Two things to fix. Then it's off to Nofunland, yah, it is so.

When she'd first driven up she'd seen Byrum sitting on the steps outside the doors, and she heard him talking to himself, it seemed, then saw the tape recorder and had started to go over to him, but he'd talked to a redneck man she thought she'd seen around town, and then had run inside.

Byrum's face was angelic and wholesome and she had thought so since she'd first met him. It was a face that contained no scheme or plan for her or anyone else, contained no devious surprises and asked nothing but actually offered something.

When she had been at Richmond Senior High, she was part

of a group who volunteered to spend time at the McLaurin Vocational Training Center working with handicapped adults trying to teach them to read. Two of those afternoons had been with Byrum. After that, she saw him now and then in town, and eventually took him to lunch on the weekends, became fond of him, saw him more often and then recently had the idea to have him record his life. The idea came from a creative writing course she'd taken where they'd read an oral history that a writer from the North Carolina mountains had helped an illiterate woman write.

"I bet your story is as good as hers," she'd told him. "We might make some money."

Now she was in the chicken plant, kind of looking for a job and waiting for her father. This is so crazy, she thought, as she went inside to talk to "Becky," a name that Gwen had given her.

"Well, if you start, you have to start on the line, deboning and trimming," Becky said. "You better read these pamphlets and look here at these pictures to see what you're getting into. It's the law that you read them, anyway."

"Yes ma'am, I will."

"There's information about how to stand and lean over and how to use your hands and all that to keep from getting tired and sore," the woman said. "You have to read that, too. The Oh-sha people require it."

She pulled a molded plastic chair across the room and out of sight of the rest of the people in the office. She faced the wall and set another chair beside her to hold the stack of abortion and right-to-life brochures. She looked from one stack of pamphlets to the other, both worries overwhelming at the moment. Something needed to be done quickly, the job, the money, the decision.

Oh God, she said to herself as she looked through the material. One of the pages showed a wet, misshapen chicken that resembled, in smeary black and white, a fetus.

The breast, the pamphlet said, may have cartilage, bone and tendons from the original detachment of the breast from the whole bird. Use a sharp knife to remove any unwanted pieces.

Everything ran together. Like a dream in split screen, like going from channel to channel, like a student hiding a book inside another one so as to be seen reading the correctly assigned one, she read from both stacks of information.

Induced abortions are caused by contraceptive drugs, such as RU 486, Methotrexate or something like that, she read, and prostaglandins, seen that word before, and there are first trimester abortions like suction and D&C, and menstrual extraction and suction-aspiration where the cervical muscle ring is paralyzed and then stretched, like the hollow into the carcass of a chicken, which is vacuumed by a tube, same as on the slaughter line.

I can't read this.

Remove the entire wing from the breast being careful to leave as much meat as possible on the breast portion, you can save the wing for stock or cook it as you wish, little old raw breast the size of that sad, floating embryo.

Of course in the 1970s and '80s, the common method was saline amniocentesis, or salt-poisoning abortions. Large needle inserted through the abdominal wall to the sac, oh my God.

Employee removes the bones from the leg and thighs, legs are brought to the employee on a conveyor located in front of employee, kind of like a parade, she reaches in front of her body, obtains a leg to be worked on and places it in front of her, the cuts consist of a stabbing cut, learn this, watch this, and slice up along the bone, breaking the leg bone at the end closest to the foot and pulling and cutting the meat away, simple, you remove the fat and gristle from the meat throw the finished meat up onto the conveyor, bones and waste are pushed into a disposal located to the right side of the work shelf.

Employees perform cuts on the deboning operation with the elbow in an elevated abducted posture. Employees use the non-cutting hand as a clamp to secure the meat during the cutting process. This requires the use of considerable finger and hand force to stabilize the meat, with a pinch grip since the hand is covered with the rubber gauntlets and the meat is slick. Continuous force by the fingers is consistent with tendon stretch and irritation. Standing a long time creates static loading on the muscles of the back and legs, leads to venous pooling of blood in legs and pressure and varicose veins.

Knives not adequate because the straight knife requires employee to assume ergonomically awkward posture. Inspector inspects finished pieces of meat and sorts them depending on degree of perfection, they reach out and feel and visually inspect, bending over at the waist. Also, she read, there is the job as leg trimmer, on the leg line.

Employees receive deboned chicken parts from conveyor belt grab parts as they pass, cutting away skin, gristle, bone and acting fast with scissors. Use of scissors and the number of repetitions and frequency of finger motions cause musculoskeletal injuries, employees should have a fifteen-minute break every two hours.

Skinner and Loader. Employee lifts tubs of chicken parts and dumps them into a tray from which they are loaded one at a time onto conveyor belt, torso flexion, nope, thigh deboner, thigh line, employee places thighs on a mandrill block with the thigh bone facing out, so employees farther down the line can remove it, employee impales thigh on two small nail-like items.

Skin puller. Pliers-like snip-device grasps skin, meat held in left hand and snip in right, skin pulled off and thrown into bin, abduction of elbow up and away from body.

Good Lord, I'm out of here. Just as soon as he shows up.

CHAPTER 20

Becky returned to the office while Gwen and Ellie waited inside the front door for the supervisor. The marinating room was a cooler place to work than over the fryers.

"You'll have to wear a sweatshirt or something," Gwen said to Ellie.

"Isn't the starting pay $5.50?"

"Yeah. Beats minimum wage."

"Which is?"

"$4.25 I think. I'm pretty sure."

"That's what I thought."

"Did you call your dad?"

"Not exactly."

"You couldn't reach him?"

She had found her father at the Peach Blossom Motel, a collection of eight pink one-room cottages built in the early 1950s. They were arranged in a semi-circle around a central cottage where the managers lived and had their office. In its early days, it was a favorite for families and young marrieds. It was now mostly used by construction workers paying $100 a week per room, two to a room, and the occasional traveler who wanted a $20 a night room.

The motel was on Business 74, which connected Hamlet and Rockingham in what had become a nearly continuous commercial district, so that, were it not for signs and the importance of history, a person might assume that the two towns were all Rockingham, though in times past, Hamlet was the larger and more prosperous city.

"Hi, girl," her father had said late the night before when she showed up. "I was hoping you'd come by."

"You still don't have your car?" she had asked.

"No."

There were no vehicles in the gravel driveway of the motel except the 1951 Ford that had been repainted as a sign as part of a plan to make the place seem retro.

"You don't know where you left it?" she had asked.

"I've been trying to figure that out all day," he had said.

He was thin, had dark, straight hair oiled lightly with Vitalis, combed back from his forehead and over the top in what some people called the 'just out' look, meaning it was a way that many white men looked who just that day had gotten out of prison. He had on shiny, black slacks, a striped Wendy's shirt, a pair of dark nylon socks that had fallen down around his ankles, and no shoes.

"Was it in Richmond County? I mean, where were you?"

"I can't remember that, either. I think it was."

Because her hair was short, she imagined she looked like him, or thought that she would when she was older. His face had thousands of miles on it, and they both, she'd realized after she'd gotten it, had tattoos on their left upper arm, his that said "82nd

Airborne," with a fist and a .45, and hers that was simply a tiny red heart with an arrow through it, but no name.

The television was on and was getting a late-night weather forecast. Fuzzy, dotted color images of maps and weather fronts across the country played in the corner of her eyes as she looked at her father, trying to see the difference between herself and him, and trying to determine if he was serious this time about his reformation.

The door was open and she saw lights coming toward them. An older car, what she thought was a '70s-model Lincoln, sunk low to the ground not from style or cool, but from metal fatigue and worn out suspension, parked beside her own car.

"Who's that?" she asked.

"It might be Robbie. I think it is. Do you have the money?"

No one got out of the car. The headlights went out and the interior went dark.

"I want you to come to Capital Foods tomorrow."

"Where?"

"The chicken plant."

"Tomorrow?"

"Let me pick you up early tomorrow morning and come get a job there. Gwen says they'll hire you. You have to do this. I'll be there."

"The chicken plant?"

"Yes, Dad. It's the kind of place you could probably work drunk and they wouldn't care."

"That's not nice. I don't drink during the day. Except on weekends."

"Well, you seem unenthusiastic. I want to make you understand you got to do this."

"You'll be there?"

"Yes."

"All right. Did you bring the money? Why will you be there?"

"Promise?"

"Yes. But don't pick me up. Robbie'll take me on his way to work. He's going to stay here tonight with me."

"I only paid for one person. They'll charge me if someone else stays here."

"They don't care. But don't come by. You don't want to drive all this way. I'll be there."

"You don't even know what time and you're promising to be there?"

"Now you sound like your mother."

"Be there at seven. Will you?"

"I said I would."

"I'm trying to help. But listen to me. This is the last time."

"You've always helped me. And I'll pay you back this time. I told the people you'd have the money. I'll pay you back. I swear it."

"Why do you owe it?"

"I don't want you to know."

"Is it for the courts? Is it a fine?"

"Forget it."

"I don't have it," she said.

She walked through the screenless, open doorway and up to the Lincoln. The windows were faux-smoked with black vinyl stick-ons and rolled up even though it was still in the mid-eighties and humid. The engine was off. She peered against the glass but only saw her muted reflection and the lights from her father's room behind her. She knocked on the window. The engine started. Four fingers with bitten nails and bruised ends peeked over the top of the glass as it moved downward a half an inch and then stopped. The man then pulled hard while holding the electric button and finally got it lowered enough to make eye contact with her.

"You're to take my dad to the chicken plant tomorrow morning before seven," she had said.

"Where. Tyson?"

"Capital. On Bridges Street."

"Sure."

"You hear me? I mean be there at seven."

She had almost believed her father might do it this time, for her, because he was in real trouble, and she had therefore been hurt this morning when he had not shown up. The hurt was significant because it was the hurt of family and father and daughter and long-standing in its accumulation, like a bad leg that snapped or went weak over many years when the same action, the same hopeful action—hopeful that it wouldn't hurt this time— was performed.

"I got word to him," she told Gwen as they waited, "that he needed to come by today and get a job. He'll show up later. I'm pretty sure. I'm going to wait around for him, anyway."

"Oh. So you're not really going to work here? You're just waiting for him? What's the story?"

"Jay," the big redneck yelled close to Ellie and Gwen. "Come on back here, boy."

Buck glanced at the two women and nodded to Gwen and then, without either trying to hide it or not aware enough to know he should hide it, looked Ellie up and down so thoroughly and in such detail she could almost feel his eyes rolling on her body like they were actually rolling across her skin, over her breasts, down her legs, a physical sensation, that tactile and oppressive.

"Hello there, little lady," he said. "New here?"

"I'm not here," she said.

"Leave her alone," Gwen said.

"Did you call for me, Buck?" Jay asked. He said hello to Ellie and nodded to Gwen.

Ellie sat on a metal cart that was low to the ground and had rubber casters under it. The wheels were mounted so that they could turn 360 degrees. She pushed herself back and forth in a small circle while she waited to be taken to the work area. She peered into the room through a door opening and saw the marinating area, which, as far as she could tell, was walled off from the other rooms except for one narrow doorway.

The room, with straps and cutting implements hanging from the walls and ceiling by rubber cords and ropes, looked like a torture chamber from a horror movie except that instead of being dim or darkly scary, it was as bright as a surgical theater. She leaned in and squinted. She looked at her hands. They were blue-white in color, as if the fluorescent tubes were under skin or inside her veins.

She got back on the cart and rolled toward another room. People looked up at her but no one spoke. The air was cold. The floor was splotchy and smeared and appeared blood-soaked. It looked as if many creatures had been killed in there, when, in fact, none had. The plant dealt only with parts of creatures. Across the back wall was the word, Buttercup, spelled out in bricks set into the block like an inlay. The word itself was barely readable, and she remembered that this had been the ice cream factory, the very place she, as a first- and second-grader, had come with her class to get free cups of ice cream, something all the schools could do on beautiful spring afternoons, and had been doing for almost fifty years in that town, the very place where her grandmother had actually worked, and then, briefly, her mother. She had forgotten it was the same building.

She recalled how cold it was inside then, and how spotless and cheerful and full of wonder and surprises it had been, how magical it had been to walk inside that place and see the happy women in white coats and white hats making the ice cream and know that you and all your friends were going to get sample cups of whatever flavor they were running that day.

Now, instead of ice cream, there was a long, steel table that looked like an autopsy bench. It had nozzles and faucets and a trough drain built in. It stretched almost across the room. Instead of stainless steel containers of peppermint chunk delight, there were brown plastic barrels with pieces of chicken skin and yellowish bubbly fat hanging off their sides. Fire extinguishers hung on the walls like little bombs with hoses attached to them.

Different sounds that she could not identify added in one by one, as machinery came on and belts began to move and chains rattled and went taut. The lights dimmed and blinked as worn armatures and brushes and capacitor-start, once well engineered electric motors spun and heated up. There was more noise as the steel roller bearings, loose in their dry raceways, caused shafts to wobble, making what should have been the solid, comforting, steady hum of the lubricated precision of spinning wound copper wires within the magnetic cradle, uneven and faltering, rising and falling in voltage.

That was what Ellie heard, what sounded to her like the roar of a crowd, rising and falling, and on the rise as loud, it seemed as she slowly backed away from the door, as the Doppler of an approaching helicopter. It made her feel as if she herself was spinning.

V-Belts worn from years of strain and now loose on pulleys, slipped and screeched as the motors jerked into motion. The tensioners on the belts no longer pressed against them tightly, letting the belts slip. The thousands of individual components that needed to be adjusted or replaced or greased, down to the set-screws and keyways in slotted shafts, all moved at once. Everything rattled and vibrated and squealed and rumbled like any machine or human that had been severely used day in and day out, year after year.

On the flat chain conveyor, a piece of a chicken leg that was caught in the hinged portion of the chain, went around and around like part of a person on a carousel, appearing and then carried away and then appearing again, the little remnant of leg traveling the entire length of the chain from one end of the room to another, and then around again, having stuck in there long ago. It was now merely a slice of its once recognizable form, just a wagging, dingy flap of skin and bone on a endless belt, no one ever having the time to stop the machine at just the right point to take it off. That machine, once stopped during production time, was simply another emergency of repair, all focus directed on getting it back in operation to keep the product, and the workers, moving.

Everything needed to stay in motion.

The workers stood beside the belt and its movement moved them.

They took the separated components of the ancestor of the colorful jungle fowl and trimmed away the waste, their hands and arms moving in time to the belt, everything flowing past and being picked up and altered to specs and set back down and then once again, the belt moving, the hands and arms moving, the back bending, the shoulders forward, the work as endless, for those eight hours, as the circular belt itself, as endless as the invention of circular mechanical movement had forever demanded from the human tender.

"Hey, Ellie," Byrum said as he walked by carrying an armload of round tubes.

"Hey, yourself. I want to talk with you. Meet me at break time, if I'm still here," she said.

"Did you come to see me?"

She had on a jacket and her hands were pulled up inside the sleeves. She reclined on the dolly and dreamily pushed herself like a patient absentmindedly rocking back and forth, only she did it not as if she were trying to rock herself out of her mind or back into it, simply rolled this way and that way, like a child.

What a horrible, amazing place, she thought.

"JAY," Buck called from behind her. "Follow me. PDQ."

Just then a woman and a child came around the corner and Ellie recognized them but couldn't immediately recall from where. Behind them Martha trailed, talking to someone yet behind her, who turned out to be Gwen.

"Lois," Martha said, "I'm not sure this is going to fly with you know who, even though I know why you got her here. I'm sorry. You know the rules. Right sweetie?" she said with a quick nod to the child.

"I'll put her in the car," Lois said.

"They said it was okay. My teacher called. Mr. Russell said it was okay. I got the half day off. I'm doing a report on where my mom works."

The lights blinked again as the vats and body heat from the hundred employees registered on the thermostats and the air conditioning units cycled back on, the entire building, except the offices and the oil steamy cooking rooms, kept at refrigerator temperature to preserve the poultry parts that were out in the open, on tables, conveyors, in boxes and large clear bags.

"You go, girl," someone yelled across the trim room as a co-worker slipped and did a skidding kind of jiggle and jerk, which she then turned into a dance to the delight of the women lined up against the table. Their heads spun around but their hands and arms kept moving in the few seconds they looked away, and not a moment of labor was lost.

"What are we going to do?" Ellie asked.

"This is fajitas day in here," Gwen said. "We just pull loose the pieces of meat and let them go on that moving thing there into the machine and ready to cook, in that other room, and then they get coated with sauce, back over here."

"So, you use those knives?" Ellie asked, and had a vivid one second flash to the terrible images she'd been reading about. "Sharp, aren't they?"

"Nope. That's one of the problems. You can wear those gloves when you cut, but if you do, you can't feel what you're doing, and the knives are dull, so you have to push harder."

"Push harder."

"Sometimes your hands are so cold you cut yourself but don't know it until the end of the day when you thaw out."

"Why's that little girl here?"

"That machine there's supposed to chip off little pieces of meat and then what's left goes on to be filets and all that, but it won't work right. They got to fix it."

"Why's the little girl here?"

George walked by with a young black man who had a studious face, and alert, bright eyes. It was Antonio, and they were discussing, and stopped to do so in the middle of the room, Carly's presence.

"You know, if she won't be in the way and you take responsibility, then I'd say who cares," George said. "Even though me and my father said it was okay, I wish we hadn't."

"She's just like a little adult. She won't cause any trouble."

"In an hour or so, get her out. And you know, when you take her to school, you punch out. You don't do that on company time."

"No, sir."

"And you need to be in fryer room, checking on the grease. Add some more if we need it."

"I think there's something wrong in there."

"I told them to fix that on Friday. On Saturday."

"We still keeping the soybean oil at 375 degrees?"

"If you can't get it to 400."

"Yes sir."

"And catch up on the flour," he said, looking toward where Antonio would normally be filling a drum from 100-pound bags all day. "Standing here talking doesn't keep that full. Get moving."

"Yes sir."

The room beside the cutting room was the marinating and mixing room. It was to the left of where Ellie stood beside Gwen and was connected by a single doorway.

"I'm not cold," Carly said.

"So now you see just exactly what your momma does," Lois said to her as she noticed Antonio coming up behind her.

"I knew you got dirty hands doing this," Carly said. "I was wondering what made those colors in the lines in your palm and under your fingernails."

"This coating here. Mexican flavorings."

"It sometimes looks like your hands are glowing in the dark, when you come home."

Antonio waited quietly behind and slightly to the side of Lois, not wanting to startle her while she worked and not aware she was ignoring him. After a minute, he tapped her on her shoulder so lightly it barely caused her smock to reflect under his fingertips.

"Don't be sneaking up behind me," she said. "I don't like that."

"Antonio. Flour."

"Hi, little girl," Byrum said as he handed Lois a package. "They said to give you this for this afternoon," he said. "They're changing the flavors this afternoon."

"Who's that?" Carly asked.

"Flour. More flour."

A woman about sixty years old in the same shower cap-style hairnet-cover that everyone else wore, but with an apron on instead of a smock, put her arm on Antonio's and turned him toward her.

"Mr. Cotton, if you please. Can I borrow your daddy?" she asked when she saw the girl looking up at her.

* * *

At 7:30, Martha and Becky returned. Becky wore heels and a long denim skirt that caused her to look as if she had stepped into a round blue barrel. It came to her ankles. She wore a red sweater with a rolled-under turtle neck, and her hair was in a tight permanent that the beauty parlors in that part of the state seemed to use as its automatic, default style for any woman over fifty.

"I told Mr. Russell you were here and looking for work," Becky said. "He mentioned it would be a good idea for you to get experience in all the departments."

"That'd be fine. When's break? What time do we get off? Where's the door? I'm lost already."

"Can I go with her?" Gwen asked.

"Has anybody else showed up just now looking for a job?" Ellie asked.

"Send her to the fryer room first. Then to dry storage, the holding freezer, and trim room."

Byrum went by and patted Ellie on the arm.

"You seem to know him."

"He's an old friend."

"Imagine having a child like that," Becky said as they entered the fryer room. "Imagine having to raise that kind of child."

Ellie felt the heat hanging in the damp air like she was in a steaming hot shower wearing heavy clothes and with no cool or fresh air to breathe.

"Yeah," she said and lingered on that thought, actually stopping where she was as she watched Byrum disappear into the back of the building, where she could see two picnic tables with benches built onto them and a row of Pepsi machines behind. "Yeah. Imagine that."

"Morning ladies," a man wearing a Lance Cracker uniform said, wheeling past them with a hand truck loaded with boxes.

"I got two boys myself," Becky said. "You stand here with Antonio. He's taking Evelyn's place. I mean Jessie's. She's playing sick but I expect her inside in a few minutes. She's outside now."

"Sick?"

"Puking," Gwen said.

"How're you?" Antonio said.

"Great," Ellie answered. "This grease always this hot?"

"Yes ma'am. Got to be."

"It does?"

"Don't stand there in that spot," Antonio said. "That hose's leaking. Smell something?"

The little breasts parading past her looked, when they were neatly plumped, not like the breasts of humans, she thought, but like pictures she'd seen of the silicone implants, only dirtier, as if the surgeon had dropped them on the floor and picked them up and continued with the procedure, blowing off the dust, but not all of it, as the larger particles, which in this case was actually the breading, remained stuck.

Some of the patties that wiggled past her, the wiggle a function of the worn shafts, bearings and stretched chain links, jerked like shivering and floppy lumps of fleshy Jell-O. They looked like early forms of life, amoeba shaped or that weird looking shape she'd seen in movies when they showed space babies and newborn aliens floating in a liquid medium.

"Gas fumes," he said.

She looked at the hose which protruded from the bottom of the cooker and curled upward toward her calves. It pulsed and

moved a few times as the fluid passed through the bends and connectors.

Hard metal conduit, the pipes within which wiring was contained and protected, hung from the ceiling down to the tables
and conveyors, its own connector joints like knobby knees. Ellie
reached for one of these conduits and held to it like someone
standing on a subway and holding to a pole. She slid her hand
down until it contacted the coupling. She felt it inside her palm,
sweaty itself, warm from the cookers, and also greasy. She looked
at her hand and wiped it on the freshly washed apron she'd put
over her own jacket.

Beneath her was the roar of gas-fired burners that made the
noise not of a stove top cooking eye, but more like she'd imagined a blow torch sounded, or a much reduced version of a jet
engine, and she could feel the heat on her legs. She touched her
jeans at her thighs and they felt hot, as if just ironed.

She felt like she had when she'd stared at the white circle in
the ceiling, as if she were being lifted or transported, but what she
figured out was that she was getting light-headed.

I got to tell Ricky about this, she thought.

The breasts rode the escalator chain into the fryer, similar to
the way pizzas rode into an oven on a time-controlled moving
metal belt, and then rode out the other end eight minutes later,
cooked and ready to box. The pieces of chicken were transported down into the grease, sandwiched between two layers of rack
so they wouldn't float to the top or inside closed baskets, like fries
being cooked at a burger joint, a basket with a lid, submerged
until the timer went off.

"You little ladies going to have to move in a minute or two,"
Buck yelled from behind them. "And the man, here. Him, too."

He came up beside Ellie. He muscled in between the women and turned sideways so that his belly almost touched her arm.

"Just move a little bitch over that way," he said, and made to push her slightly backwards, but stopped just short of putting his hand on her. "That way."

He left the room.

"What'd he say?" Ellie asked.

"That's his trick," Lizzy said.

"He got it figured out so he can say *he said* 'just a little bit'. He some worrisome man," Lois, who had just joined this crew, said. Carly sat behind them on a pile of paper bags that were fluffy with green sweeping compound.

"He doesn't bother me," Antonio said.

"Yeah," Lois said, "not much. He's just a few minutes short of a white sheet and pointed hat, that's the truth about him."

"He won't bother you," Lizzy said. "We won't let him."

"I'm not scared of him," Antonio said. "He's just a lot a talk."

He and the women arranged the filets as fast as they came from the trim room. All the while they talked, they were, like everyone else in the plant, making production. The talk was the distraction, the reward, the magic they were casting on one another to pretend away the drudge and grit and monotony of the job.

"Hey Lance Cracker man," a big woman who was in her sixties and had worked in that same building ever since it was the ice cream plant, called out through the doorway into the break room. "You out of peanut butter cheese, you know. I eat two a day."

"Two cases, she means."

"Let me see those pictures, Lizzy. I know you got some."

Ellie kept quiet while they talked but she looked over Lizzy's shoulder to see the baby. Lance Man came through the doorway pushing the empty hand truck. Behind him, in the break room, two Pepsi machines stood side by side. One had eight clear, plastic buttons with logos of each flavor behind them, Mountain Dew, Diet Mountain Dew, and the rest, to choose from, and the other machine, an older one, had six choices. There were two Lance machines, the kind with a glass picture window showing racks of crackers and peanuts and honey buns and oatmeal cookies and little round pecan pies. When the money was inserted and choice made and the handle pulled, the item moved forward and then fell. The products looked like people did when they jumped off a cliff, slowly moving to the edge of the shelf and then suddenly dropping.

There was a door to the outside in the corner of the room. It was the same door where Charlie Russell had stabbed his hand trying to remove a wooden wedge stuffed into the panic bar by the workers to keep the door unlocked. On the ceiling were two fluorescent lights. A fire extinguisher was to the left of one of the Lance machines, and to the right of that was a coffee and milk vendor. On the floor in front of it were cracked foam cups and spilled coffee and beside the machine a trash barrel full of wrappers and cans and half-pint chocolate milk cartons.

"Look at the perfect little girl," Lois said looking at the photos. "Now you did that, you see? You made that perfect little baby."

"I did. You're right."

"God made that baby," someone said. "He just let you carry it."

"That's true," she said.

"Sweet Jesus, thank you for that healthy baby."

"Now Mr. Russell? You remember that last day before Lizzy

left?" Cecilia asked. She had red hair pulled in a long pony tail that stuck out from under her shower cap, and a fine featured, intelligent face.

"Yes."

"Well, he did something that was so strange," she said.

Ellie watched the cheerful expressions as they looked from one to the other and she listened to the woman with the red hair who was trying to tell some story, some event she'd witnessed, and she noticed again how their hands never stopped moving, and how they did what they had to do on automatic, and she tried to separate out the sounds of the equipment from the women.

She slipped her gloves off by catching them under her armpits on opposite sides, and put both her hands over her ears, cupping them like muffs to drown out the din, and moved from the end of the line to just behind Cecelia and then took her hands away because holding them like that had caused the noises to reverberate in some unexpected way that made it worse.

"He strange, anyway," someone said.

"What man ain't?"

"Well, that last day . . . ," Cecelia tried again.

"Gordon," a woman said, "had me in my car and I was driving."

"Ellie? Come on in here for a minute, would you?" Becky called from the doorway of one of the walk-in coolers. It was the size of a camper trailer. It had a set of heavy, plastic strips hanging in front of the doorway. The strips kept the cool air in, but allowed people to walk through without opening and closing a door.

"How come you driving? I don't have no memory of no man ever letting me drive while he was in the car."

"Isn't that the truth."

"He was watching how I drove because I made the mistake of telling him that the car didn't have no power."

"Uh oh."

"So I started off at a stop sign and the thing wouldn't go, and I said, 'Look here, it just won't go,' and he reached over and stomped down on top of my foot on the gas pedal and mashed me and the pedal to the floor," she said, and had to stop because she started, along with everyone else, laughing too hard to continue, "slammed that big old size 13 shoe on top of me and held my little old foot on the floor, I'm telling you, the car just took off."

"I kill that man."

"And he said you see, dopey, it won't go unless you mash the gas pedal. That's why it won't go."

"Well, old Mr. Russell," Cecelia said, continuing her interrupted story, "was standing right there and I saw him almost put his hand right into that grease. I swear he did. His fingers. It seemed like he put them in there."

"His fingers?"

"His fingertips. It looked like he was cooking them. Like he was cooking his fingers, or about to."

"Then what?"

"Then he did like this."

A supervisor came in as she finished her story and imitated what Charlie had done. She leaped backwards three times and then slipped on the final landing and ended up on the floor.

"Playing again, Cecelia?" he asked.

"No sir, I wasn't really."

He took out a pad of paper. "One-half demerit, 8 A.M., Sept. 3, 1991," he said.

CHAPTER 21

8 A.M.

Charlie was not feeling well and had there been golf supervisors overseeing his game that morning, he'd have received demerits. Even though his surroundings were expansive and his vistas were unencumbered and the colors of his life, at that moment, were lush and verdant, he was uneasy.

"We have the course to ourselves, or nearly so," his friend Paul said.

They surveyed the perfectly cut fairway ahead of them. To their left, on another fairway, two sprinkler heads emerged from the ground and sprayed invitingly cool well water in arcs a hundred feet to either side. The water rose into the air and fell in a design that was as carefully reproduced as landscape sculpture, a process that had been worked out by engineers so that even the watering function of the golf course was a thing of beauty.

It was as if the land itself, the courses, this one and those all over the Sandhills and beyond, had become not simply places to play golf, but parks in the manner and style of royalty, where life rolled along as smoothly and silently as the electric carts that moved, relative to the lurch and noise of the auto, like magic. Men and women strolled in a form of clean and ordered experience within nature, naturalists in motion, gracious and familial, the gestures, clothes and cadence of their acts all understood and repeated—comforting, safe and richly earned.

"Maybe we're too early," Charlie said.

"They've watered this first part," his friend said. "We're fine."

Charlie had more than a million dollars in high-interest debt. A half a dozen lawsuits followed him like crows everywhere he went, he often said, beaks open, cawing and eating at him. Workers at plants he'd bought in other states had sued him, and the plan for vertical integration had failed.

"You're kind of distracted," Paul said. "Shall we go on to work or continue to play? You call it."

"Let's play."

Back at the clubhouse, where carts with tan canopies and royal blue logos were parked, a machine with black rollers bumped across the parking lot where the grass stopped and the asphalt began. Behind it a speeding lawnmower with spinning reels whirled around in turns so tight they looked centrifugal, almost as if there would be an increase in G forces from the speed, and the young man driving looked like he was playing rather than working, as if he was on a bumper car happily out of control.

"I'm making nothing," Charlie mumbled and fiddled with the clubs stuck down into the expensive leather sheath like rockets stuffed into a launcher pod, like rifles nosed down in a carrier, implements of war and the hunt now turned into a game, the sword, the rifle, the spear, the rocket, the bomb, now mutated into the game of golf.

"You make more money by accident than I make trying

hard," his partner said. "You get more money out of the lowly hen than anyone could have ever imagined."

"Roosters."

"I see those trucks leaving your plant all day long."

"Right."

"There's one backed up to the dock right now. I passed it early this morning. The driver was asleep in the cab. You're paying the man to sleep. Nice of you to do that."

"That's all contract hauling," Charlie said. "They squeeze me as bad as anyone."

The greens were wet and therefore slow this early in the morning, so few people were on the course and Charlie and Paul, who owned a chain of car washes located throughout the Sandhills, could get a quick eighteen holes in and still be at work by ten.

"Twenty dollars says you don't make that putt," Paul said. "How about it?" he asked after a pause during which his friend was again off somewhere. "Twenty?" he asked, and tapped Charlie on the shoulder.

Charlie picked up his hat and looked across the fairway, and his eyes, to Paul, who'd been in the second world war himself, had that stare he'd seen when soldiers had crossed the line between being there and never being there again.

"You owe me twenty," Charlie said.

Charlie had been slipping back to his war time experiences every day for months. The memories were vivid and had come to stay beginning with the Memorial Day weekend and were still there this morning after Labor Day.

"I haven't had any fun since I was just back from the war," he said and was lost in the thought of all he'd had to learn back then, how it seemed, now, that nothing was going right. He had rarely been a day without worry in almost fifty years.

A bomber dropped forty to fifty tons of bombs in its life during the war. It was calculated that would produce, when released in populated areas, between 4,000 and 8,000 homeless. Not all killed, but homeless.

"Since then?" Paul asked, trying to stay in the conversation. "No fun since then?"

He was at two thousand feet. The target indicator bombs would explode at seven hundred feet. If he calculated wrong, he would be incinerated. They would explode on him. He looked at the railway lines and to the left of them were his marking points. He'd studied the maps carefully. He called out on the radio frequency he'd been assigned that he was beginning his run. A photographic connector synchronized the pictures of the release of the thousand-pound target bomb.

"Hadn't we earned the right to enjoy the fruits of our labor by making a profit?" Charlie asked, coming back to the present.

"You bet."

Zero hour was nine minutes away. His fuel tank capacity allowed him another thirty minutes over the area. He wanted to be around to witness the attack. A plane with navigation lights appeared. Messerschmitt 110.

"Where's my ball?" Charlie asked. "Where'd it go?"

"In the sand."

The De Havilland Pathfinder plane was the best low altitude twin engine precision bomber the British had, and the fastest, which is why they also used it as the P.R. 1 Photo Reconnaissance plane. Its Merlin engines were so powerful and reliable the U.S. used them.

From the sky, in enemy territory, almost every town looked the same—the rivers, the roads, the mountains, the farmland—all often looked the same. Bomber crews had, early in the war before navigation beams were improved, bombed targets 100 miles off their intended destination, not ever knowing they were in the wrong place. He could have just marked the wrong city. No Chamber of Commerce put up signs during the war on rooftops advertising the names of their towns.

It had been decided that it would take a year between mid 1942 and 1943 to make a third of the German population homeless. The Germans had started this population terror, and now they were going to get it back.

"I believe the battery's about dead in this cart."

The bombing death rate was 3/4 of a person killed per ton of bombs. That meant it took slightly more than a ton of bombs to kill one single person. If a formation of planes dropped a hundred tons of bombs, many of them exploded in open places or, if on target, did a great deal of property damage, but that many bombs would statistically only have killed 75 people. Many more people died in shelters, however, trapped where the fumes, flames and lack of oxygen were inescapable.

"Hell," Paul said. "It's not dead. I was mashing the top of that hump in the floor right there, thinking it was the accelerator pedal. You got me going nuts like you."

The British, with men like Charlie Russell attached to them from the Eighth Air Force, perfected the art of population bombing during the war. By this time in the war, much of the German Air Force was destroyed.

"I'm going to buy my own cart," Paul said. "You want to go in with me?"

CHAPTER 22

8:15 A.M.

Lance Man came through one more time with an armload of rectangular boxes.

"Peanut butter and cheese."

A freezer door was open to Ellie's right, pushed back to the wall. It had a release handle on the inside. It looked like all the doors to walk-in freezers in the movies she'd seen where the people get locked inside by thieves.

"Hate to be locked in by that thing," she said.

"They never close it," Gwen said. "The curtains keep the cold in."

There were metal shelves on each of three walls, with boxes of chicken parts. The sides were greasy. They had that same odor she'd smelled throughout the plant.

"The cardboard is waxed."

The big man who'd eyed Ellie reappeared, stepping out of the dark quickly, catching everyone off guard and looming over them in an uncomfortable way.

"Slide over, little ladies," Buck said. "We got to fix that leak."

"Can't you do it tonight?" one of them asked. "We can't stop. We'll make nothing if we do. And quit sneaking up on us all the time."

"Nobody's stopping. You keep going."

"The belt'll stop."

"Use the manual baskets. We'll keep the burners on."

"We ain't supposed to do that."

"We do what we got to do, and listen up. If this repair takes longer than a few minutes, you ladies find something to do and if I see any of you not doing nothing, punch out until this gets fixed."

"That's a double negative," Ellie said.

"How's that?"

"Where's the leak?" Jay asked.

"There," Buck said. "Fix it."

"With what?"

"That part that came in from Central Hydraulics."

"Why don't you do it?" Cecelia asked.

"You just do your job, girl," Buck said.

"Why don't you do yours? Jay got enough to do."

"I can do it," Jay said.

"Yeah, Buck, use those big arms of yours for something else besides picking up Quarter-Pounders. You do something."

"You girls do your job. This ain't none of your business."

"You should have fixed that last week," someone said. "I've stepped in that oil a dozen times."

"Where's the part?" Jay asked.

Buck kicked at the new hose right behind him.

"I have to turn off the burners," Jay said. "That's what the regulations say."

"You don't turn nothing off," Buck said.

"I got to turn off the pump," Jay said. "Regulations."

"He got to turn off the pump," Cecelia said and all the rest of the women joined in with a chorus of, "Yeah, he got to turn off the pump."

"Figure it out, boy," Buck said. "Just don't turn off those burners or the pump. It takes too long to get that oil up to temperature. You want to keep everyone out of work all morning?"

"Where's the pump switch?"

"Leave it on. Just close the valve to that section of hose. You know that. You know you do. Leave the pump on."

The hydraulic hose ran the conveyor belts. It worked similar to any hydraulically-operated device, like the power steering in a car. A pump built up pressure and sent the oil through lines. When the oil passed over a device, it turned it. The pressure of the oil pushed against the gears and the gears rolled over and the belt moved and the people moved and the breasts and patties paraded across the room and into the hot grease.

The problem with hydraulic devices was that it took enormous amounts of pressure to move the belts. The hoses, which had to be flexible to follow the twists and turns to get to the various parts of the machine, developed leaks, especially at the connectors, just like garden hoses did. Home water systems had between 40 and 80 pounds of pressure, and hydraulic systems like the one in the chicken plant, had 800 to 1500 pounds of pressure.

Jay plugged in a work light and shone it on the leaking hose. He moved his hand along it until he felt a stream of oil coming out as mist.

Nearby, the big circular gas burners roared in open flames,

heating the bottoms of the fryer tanks which were filled with soybean oil, different from the oil in the hydraulic lines.

He found a valve and turned it. His section of hose immediately stopped leaking and for a moment he forgot exactly where the pin prick had been. He looked at the pool of oil under the bent section and realized it was where the hose, too long to fit properly out of the way under the vat, stuck out where the workers stood, so that they constantly stepped on it.

"What in the hell is going on here?" George asked.

"Fixing the hose, boss," Jay said from under the fryer.

"We working," someone else said. "Working and talking."

"Mostly talking," he said.

"I'm going to walk out that door right now," Evelyn said when he was out of sight. "Right this minute."

"You are not. Where else you going to work?"

"I'll work somewhere. I can cook chicken at Bojangles same as cook it here."

"Right. For a dollar an hour less."

"And work whatever shifts they tell you. Come in now, you show up, they tell you they said tomorrow, you show up then, next day they tell you you're on the night shift. Drive me crazy," someone said.

"That's true. At least here, you do the same hours every day."

"I'm going out that door right now," Evelyn said again. "I'll be out of here by break time. You wait and see."

Jay got off the floor and leaned backwards, stretching and getting the kinks out of his spine from bending double.

"I got it," Jay said. "I think I got it figured out."

The old hose lacked the quick coupler connections that more

modern lines had. This line joined the other line nearby with a brass female piece that screwed onto a brass male receiver. He put a wrench on one end and one on the other end and pushed them in opposite directions until the joint broke free. Residue of the remaining oil spilled out and ran across the concrete slab toward his shoes, where it seeped under his soles before he could get out of the way.

"I would forget that was bound to happen."

He soaked up the spill and then put dry rags under where he was working and at the other end of the hose, where a similar connector would have to be wrenched apart.

"Fry that chicken," he said to his wife and the rest of the women, making fun of the supervisors' admonitions, and then separately to Ellie, who was standing behind everyone looking curious. "A mess, huh?" he asked her. "You coming to work here?"

"This whole place is a mess," she said. "Can I help you? May I?"

At the other end of the hose he loosened the same type joints and then folded the 18-inch-long hose in half, inadvertently squeezing out more of the oil when he did, and then mopped that up and tied the folded hose with a rag so that it was only nine inches long, bent double. He took off his hat and hung it on a protruding bolt on the metal leg nearby.

"No thanks, I can do it."

She liked him, the way he talked and moved and how he looked, how sincere and sweet he seemed, and also how completely out of place he seemed in this chicken plant. She was also fairly sure he didn't have a clue what he was doing and she wanted to lie down under there with him and help. She wondered why she'd never seen him around town, or remembered him from school. He was older, but not by many years.

"I've worked on my car enough to know a little," she said.

He removed the new hose from the box. It was longer than the one he'd just taken off. He looked at both ends to see if the fittings would match, and held them against their mates, noting the threads and couplings.

"Looks right," he said, and then noticed the women weren't watching him. He'd imagined that they were all still looking his way and keeping up with the repairs.

"Looks right," Ellie said.

"I hadn't ever done this particular kind of thing," he said to her after she leaned over to see better under the vat. "Normally I work on the electric motors, the forklift, pallet skidder, that kind of stuff."

"Normally," she said, "I don't spend much time underneath chicken fryers, myself."

"Normally," he said back and laughed, "I would kind of wish to say the same. I don't intend to spend too much time around here, period, if things turn out right this afternoon."

"Likewise," she said and patted him on the head.

His hair was sandy colored and clean and she could smell some familiar shampoo or shaving lotion on him, and without realizing she was doing it, she patted his hair lightly, stroked it a few times, and then kept on because once she touched it, she wanted to feel it again, feel the way it was against her skin. It may have been because his hair was something clean and inviting and delicate finally, after the time she'd spent touching pieces of cold, skinned and deboned meat.

It may also have just been because she liked him. She didn't think about it. She just stroked his hair and left her fingers on his head too long, longer than anyone might even have done by accident. She realized it too late, and looked at Lizzy, and then across the room at the other women.

"Can I help you?" Lizzy asked. "Have you got some problem?"

Ellie apologized and walked out of the room.

The husband and wife looked at each other, one embarrassed and the other perturbed.

"I didn't do anything," Jay said.

Ellie wandered past workers she hadn't met and toward a cold region of the building. It was where refrigerated trucks loaded and unloaded. She stood on the edge of the concrete slab and rocked back and forth on a metal ramp that had been slid forward onto the back of an empty trailer.

There was darkness there that should have led out from the building into freedom, but was, instead, a dead end. As her eyes got used to the dimness, she realized there were two scratched, road-filthy skylights built into the trailer's ceiling and after a minute or so, her eyes got used to the dark. A compressor was mounted on the trailer and it sounded like a lawnmower running wide open.

Two empty cardboard boxes were on the floor. She picked them up. They were coated with the same hard, shiny and sticky finish, both inside and out. She carried them into the warehouse.

The air there was also stale, as if the smell of skinned bird cadavers had seeped into the masonry walls. She carried the boxes at her sides until she returned to the processing area. She set them against the bags along the wall where Carly sat.

"Are you learning anything?" she asked the girl.

Lizzy had rejoined the women she'd been working with and

they were quiet a second too long when she returned, which told her they'd been watching and listening to her and her husband.

"Well, he does have the prettiest hair," Lizzy said. "I can't keep my own hands out of it."

They laughed and with the laughter that acted for them like the pressure relief valve of any charged system, the pace and sense of normal returned, the same way it did in church when a startling revelation was observed, and the congregation sighed or hummed, yes Lord, or Amen, or That's Right.

Jay continued to work, and droplets of warm oil seeped out the ends of the existing fittings when he removed the deteriorated sections. The shut-off at the junction behind him held the pressurized fluid from blasting out like a cut artery in a human body, which would have, not surgically clamped off, spurted with each heartbeat.

"I need some Teflon tape or pipe dope," he said to Buck, who had returned.

"Use the tape. That leak'll dilute the dope before you can get it threaded back tight."

"Okay."

"What're you standing there for, girl?" Buck asked Ellie, who had moved from the back of the room and toward the group as they walked away from the table and pan.

"Are you working here or not? Because if you are, then do something. And if you're not, then get out of the building."

The women who'd been in the fryer room had moved to the other side where another conveyor deposited flash frozen breasts onto a table and where another woman was alone in a two-person job, trying to catch them as they came through an opening in a wall, and insert them one-by-one into separate clear bags.

After settling the breast into the bottom of the bag, she flipped the open edge over itself and ran it through a heat sealing machine.

"I'm going CRAZY here," she yelled when she saw the group coming her way.

The women were beside her now and worked on the back-log of flash frozen filets that made a mound that almost reached up to the opening in the wall.

Jay held an end of the fittings with a wrench that he chocked firmly against the floor by laying his leg across it so that he had both hands free to get the moveable threaded female end started. He lay on his back in hydraulic fluid and chicken fat and a mixture of dust and cold soybean oil as thick as Vaseline.

"Finished?" he heard someone ask and saw George standing over him.

"A few more minutes."

"Are you sure?"

"I don't know. I may have to bleed the line. Depends."

"Don't turn that friggen burner off. You want to cost me a whole day?"

"I didn't."

"That oil's got to stay at least 375."

"I know, sir. It's there."

It was so hot working next to the big gas burner that Jay felt like his back was about to burst into flame. Every now and then he'd feel his shirt to see if it might be on fire.

"Tony almost set his hair on fire on that thing," Byrum said, swinging by the work site on his way to another room. "Be careful."

"I wish I had the time to be."

"What's that?" Buck asked.

"What?"

"That," he said and dragged Jay backwards by one leg, like pulling a dead deer out of the bushes, until he was free of the fryer unit. "That damn mess sticking out there."

The new hose Central Carolina Hydraulics sent was not just a little too long. It was so long it snaked out from under the unit like a noose or snare. It looped so wide that a human could step into the middle of it and fall forward into the vat of cooking oil.

"Well, that's what they sent," Jay said. "Isn't this the part they sent?"

"Shove it under there out of the way. You can't have that shit sticking out like that. Standing on it'll just bust it open again."

"I'll try."

"Them damn women'll be all over that. They can't even reach the edge if they have to stand behind it. Bend it under there."

Jay folded the hose inward. It would neither flex that much nor would it pivot where it was connected on each end.

"It won't go. Maybe I can tuck it behind this leg."

"Do that, and I'll open the valve."

Buck watched Jay bend the hose against one of the fryer's legs. When he turned on the valve and the pressure built up the hose sprang back to its original position even with Jay's hand on it. It hit the floor so fast it trapped his hand under it and bruised his knuckles against the old concrete slab that was by now, since concrete hardened more and more with the years, as unforgiving as a granite tombstone.

"Damn, boy. You made a igger mess out of that, damn if you didn't."

Jay bent his fingers back and forth. He picked some torn skin off his knuckles and flipped it onto the floor. He also looked behind them hoping none of the African Americans had heard Buck's clever way of saying the insult without actually saying it.

"It ain't my fault it's too long," Jay said.

"Cut a section out of the middle and put a connector in there and make it the right length."

"I've never done that."

"You've seen me."

"Yeah. I mean, I know the steps, but I hadn't never done it."

"I got to look at the compressor unit on that flash box," he said. "Get what you need and I mean quick and fix it and I mean fast."

Jay returned with the coupler and a hack saw which cut only on the backward pull, and then abruptly stopped and knocked himself in his forehead with his palm. He had forgotten to shut off the valve. Had he kept slicing the oil would have spurted out like the cut artery.

He made another cut eighteen inches away from the first, and then removed that section. He put the two remaining ends against one another and saw that once they were made into a continuous hose in their shortened length, they would lay under the fryer unit out of the way of the workers' feet.

In a dark corner of the building, George watched both the work on the fryer, and across the building, the opening in the wall for the trash compactor. He had watched the new woman wander into the trailer and then back out, and had seen her carry, not something into it, as he had suspected she would be doing, but boxes back out, which, as he could see, were empty.

The compactor was squeezed against pliable rubber bumpers attached to the perimeter of the big door opening. They were there because they protected the walls from being crushed when a trailer backed into them and also because they provided a seal, similar to the one around a refrigerator door, to keep the cool air inside, the insects outside, and allow the product to be loaded while kept at the proper temperature.

The compactor didn't fit the opening as well and thoroughly as a refrigerated trailer would have. There was ten inches of daylight and open space above it and beside it because the compactor was smaller than a trailer.

As George watched, Jessie appeared with two boxes at her sides, the way Ellie had carried hers, but these boxes were flap sealed, that is, the flaps were folded in onto one another so they remained closed. He saw her toss them into the compactor, but there was method and calculation to how she tossed them, and it said everything to him.

She threw them far toward the back, using both hands to throw each, so that they landed near the exterior hatch doors. She threw them so hard, in fact, that her wig, which was the color of damp sand and cigarette smoke, slipped.

The wig fell off her head. It landed in a brightly illuminated slice of sunlight coming in from above the compactor.

Slouching and sliding her feet rather than picking them up so that the heels of her rubber boots flopped up and down because they were too big for her, she repositioned her wig and ambled toward her work site.

"Jessie," George said.

He stepped out of the shadows.

"Mr. Russell. What you hiding like that for?"

"I knew it was you."

"Me what?"

"You're finished around here."

"What's that? What you talking about?" she asked. "I don't know what you talking about," she then said as she started past him, but was stopped by his hand on her arm. "And don't you touch me. You don't got the right to touch me."

"I saw what you threw into the compactor."

"Those boxes?"

"Let's me and you go outside and look at them."

"I ain't going outside or anywhere with you. And how come you think you can tell which boxes is mine from all the other boxes in there? Huh? Ask me that, how about it."

She pulled away from him.

"And where is your cap? Jessie, you're in violation of everything. Go get your damn shower cap."

He hurried toward a door marked exit in faded, stenciled paint. He grabbed the handle. He turned it without even slowing down, ready to fling the door open and get the evidence.

"Damn," he yelled. "Damnation and hell."

He, himself, had double locked that door just a few weeks ago. He had locked it because it was too convenient for the employees to get to the parking lot where the compactor was near, easiest, then, for them to transfer what they'd stolen.

He hurried back through the rooms, having to travel half the building to get to an unlocked door at the front. Once outside, he ran to the rear and fished out the boxes and saw they were full of frozen filets.

"You're fired," he said to Jessie, as she worked along side of her friends. "You get your time card in and don't come back."

"I didn't put nothing in that dumpster," she said. "You can't prove I did. That thing's full of boxes."

"You just leave now," he said. "Just get your stuff together and leave, and don't walk out of here with another thing that belongs to us, not the boots, not the cap, not the apron, nothing."

"These boots be mine."

The women had gone even more quiet than they had when they'd witnessed Ellie petting Jay's hair. As soon as George left, however, they crowded around Jessie.

"What's he talking about?"

"He can't fire you."

"What'd you do?"

"We'll all quit. We'll show him. We'll all walk out. Right now."

"I can't lose this job," she said while her friends hugged her. "I just can't. I be so much in debt. Lord knows, I got so much debt."

"Maybe Buck can help you out," one of the women said, and then, because of how many looks she got from the group, realized she had put her foot in her mouth by suggesting that they knew about that arrangement. "I mean, maybe someone can. Mr. Ellis or someone."

"Lord, I ain't leaving. I just can't leave. I can't work nowhere else. This is all I know. Chickens is all I know."

"You can work at Tyson," the same woman said, and then got another round of looks and gestures, having forgotten she'd been fired from there before she had come to Capital.

"You just keep on working, honey. We'll think of something."

"I'm not leaving now. He can't cheat me out of whats I made today. He can't. I'll work right until the very last minute," she said.

"Ain't no work for people like us but here," someone said. "Not nowhere around these parts."

"Not in this town."

Ellie had looked out the front door to see if her father had showed up and then had wandered into the room where chopping raw chicken began. It was where the big drum that Antonio kept full of flour was bolted to the floor and which had to be fed by him once every 20 or 30 minutes.

He dumped a hundred pounds into the drum as Ellie watched. A cloud spread across the room and settled onto everyone's face and cap and into the flickering light bulbs. Not only that, but because of the sudden burden put on the machine from the weight of the added ingredients, the belts running the drum screeched like the slipping fan belts of a car, only louder and longer. The sound bounced off the ceramic walls and magnified so that the continuing reverberations met the oncoming newly produced screeching from the belts and for the thirty seconds that it took the machine to catch up with the load, no one could talk or be heard.

That room was set up like a child's playground where there was a pattern and route to be followed from one climbing or crawling or swinging device to another. At the head of the room was the grinder, where two women dumped raw chicken into a hopper that looked like a chipper that tree services used, only this one was upright, so that the chute faced the ceiling. The raw chicken was hurried to the women by men on electric forklifts. They carried barrels that they deposited beside the women who then leaned into them to get the pieces out, disappearing from the waist up and breathing in the raw smell so that most of the time whoever worked there learned to hold her breath when diving in. The ground chicken then wiggled along a conveyor to the blender, which added spices, preservatives, flavorings or color.

"Don't come in here," Gwen said to Ellie, who was looking at her as she was at the breader.

"Huh?"

"Don't come inside this mess," she yelled over the noise. "Just wait there. You'll get lost trying to find me."

From the breader the patties went into another fryer, not the one being repaired, but a similar one with an open vat of boiling soybean oil. They came out the other end and followed a conveyor to the flash-freezing room.

All of this meant that the rooms were so maze-like in their machinery configurations, that when it was time for break or lunch, it took the people working within the conveyor lines a minute or so to wind around out of them to the free area along the walls, which then led, eventually, to the other rooms, which then led, by a door here and a door there, to the break room where the bathrooms and picnic tables were.

"I'm not going to wait anywhere," Ellie yelled, and the other women looked up from what they were doing and listened to the conversation

"What do you mean?"

"I'm leaving. I can't do this. I got to figure something else out. He's not going to show up."

"You can't do it?" someone yelled above the noise. "No one can. But we do."

"Work is work," an older woman said.

"That's right."

"You get used to it. Like everything in life."

"Don't leave," Gwen yelled above the noise, which had risen as more machines within the building came on. "Wait until break time, at least. At nine-thirty. Okay? Please?"

In the fryer room in the middle of the building, Jay used a special tool to squeeze the male ends onto the hose. He repeated, once more, the wrench trick on trapping one against the floor with his leg so that he could maneuver the other one with his free hands and he tightened up the new joints.

The hose now tucked neatly under the fryer, hanging of its own strength and length within the legs of the device and out of the way of feet and the movement of hand trucks and fork lifts. The hose now sat in place beside the other hoses and adjacent to the narrow, rectangular gas burner that had been roaring bluish-yellow flames all the time he'd been working.

"You got it?"

"Yes sir."

"Then turn it on and get the women back in here," George said.

"We'll get it running right now," Buck said, miraculously appearing, Jay thought, at the very minute he'd finished, as if he'd been watching from somewhere, not doing anything at all but waiting.

It was almost 8:30.

"Get the girls back in here. Double time."

Jay started in their direction but Buck waved him back.

"Pick up the tools and rags. Set everything into the boxes the way they came. I'll get them."

"All right."

"And re-check the joint when you open the valve. Put your hand all around it and feel for anything, even if it's a mist."

In the room where meat from the flash-freezer dumped onto the table and where everyone had gone to help, Buck positioned himself directly behind the women who were all facing away. He took a two-foot section of angle iron and slammed it down on a metal table top. The result was so sudden and unexpected half the people in the room screamed and started evacuating and the other half caught their breath and spun around expecting to see a forklift crashing toward them.

"Ladies, now that I have your attention," he said.

"Screw you, Mr. Ellis," one of the women said.

"You bastard."

"Now that I have your attention, it's time to move back to your places."

The women hid Jessie as they walked into the room and then had her work in front of them and off toward the wall where the light was dimmer so the bosses wouldn't see that she was still there.

"It's not running," someone said, looking at the track. "Unless I've gone blind from what Ellis did back there."

"That belt is not moving," another said, looking Buck Ellis right in the face. "What do you do around here but run your damn mouth," she added.

"I'll run something into you if you don't shut up," he said.

"Yeah, and I'll tell my husband you said that."

"Here it comes," Jay said. "I'm turning it back on now."

The hose pulsed. The oil flowed through the new length and fittings and the conveyor moved. The women returned to work and the men stood side by side for a moment while Jay felt around the new joints.

"You got it? Is it fixed?"

"I think it's still leaking," Jay said, and looked at his hand in the light where a line of oil stretched across his palm like a faint crease.

CHAPTER 23

"What time is it? Must be something going on. My watch stopped," Paul said. They rode the path down the edge of the fairway. "It's a good watch, too."

Both men wore yellow trousers, but Charlie wore an orange knit shirt and Paul a blue. Both shirts had been woven in the Sterntex mills in Charlotte, owned by a refugee family from Nazi Germany.

"People don't know hard times," Charlie said, still halfway between the present and the past. "Give me a good veteran any day. He knows."

"Why'd my watch stop?"

"I don't know why anything happens anymore."

Parachute flares had been initially dropped to light the way for the hundreds of bombers that followed. High-explosive bombs, set barometrically to burst at two to three thousand feet above the ground, would illuminate the targets with green light. Others burst in red.

Flying above all the color made for a sight for young Charlie Russell so beautiful that what followed seemed like it couldn't be about death and terror and the gray and brown dust of destruction.

"Maybe," Paul said, eerily and innocently paralleling his golfing buddy's mind, "they dropped the A bomb and we don't know. We're just playing golf and the damn A bomb's been dropped. My watch's stopped and the whole damn world's been bombed. And we're playing golf. I kind of like that idea. He died with his putter in his hand. I like that, don't you, Charlie?"

"What?"

Charlie's recon and marker plane swooped in toward the stadium and rail yards at 200 miles an hour, going below seven hundred feet, its camera flashing. He saw a steam locomotive pulling passenger cars free from the fire, red marker flares in brilliant crimson everywhere below him. He and his fellow pilots had to clear the area quickly as the bombers were coming in. He had to fly above them, and then come down and photograph the devastation, or what they all hoped would be devastation.

"I can't chip worth crap," Paul said.

The Mosquitoes the marker pilots flew were unarmed. The guns defending the city were silent. Charlie saw people running in all directions. The big four-engine Lancasters and Liberators could bomb from lower altitudes without the anti-aircraft guns. He saw a bright, blue flash and knew an electrical power installation had been hit.

"Some of them are okay. I got some good ones," Charlie said.

"Some of what? Who?"

The 4,000-pound bombs, designed to smash windows and rip off the roofs of buildings a thousand years old, now fell. The Germans lit a fire to a decoy marker site. They never realized when they designed the sites that a burning city from above was a chaotic mess, plumes and boiling clouds of smoke, bursting high explosives, and everything untidy and without clear definition. The German decoy sites were built in perfect rectangles.

The marker pilots dropped yellow cancellation bombs on those sites and those cancellation bursts burned an oddly rich and pastel yellow that was the same color as their golfing trousers now fifty years later, a time so far removed that the green course was, he remembered, a color he rarely saw unless he created it within a burning city, unless he bombed something that burned green, something with sulfur in it.

"I pray I can keep it going," he said, getting into the cart. The taste and smell of the last of the biscuits he had bought driving to the course brought him back to the present.

"Yep. Whatever."

They finished their chicken biscuits, enjoying the breast filet that likely had been processed in his factory and then shipped to Hardees' warehouses and then back to Hamlet and to the restaurant just up the street from where it began its life torn from a breast by hard-working women, or formed up by one of Charlie's machines to look as if it had been, the filet mignon of the working class.

The flavor of the breaded chicken filet combined with the biscuit batter and buttered top was better than anything most men had eaten in all the years of the war overseas. That wonderfully good.

They drove their cart over the fertilized hills and past the semi-tropical abundance of growth along the edges toward the next tee. Some of the undulations in the course had been man-made because the land was often too flat in that part of the state for a proper hill, even though it was called the Sandhills.

Earlier, just before they got there, the sprinklers had come on according to their automated sensors and timers. For now, there would never be anymore dying vistas of grass and trees in the golfers' world. It was the lush life, lush in the belly of the men and women, and on the land. The players popping the little round projectiles into the air which then fell to earth like neat, perfect and very expensive pieces of shrapnel, had earned the right to walk the earth in the sweet and peaceful paths of golf and friendship and the pastoral poetry of success and safety.

"Where is it?"

The city had never been bombed. They would give it the full Hamburg treatment. First the windows and roofs were broken by high explosives. Then the incendiaries would set fire to the houses whipping up the sparks. Those sparks would rain through the opened roofs and windows, setting fire to the carpets, furniture, and exposed wood. The Germans had put fire resistant coatings on the framing of their attics and on the roofing that was not already tile or metal. It didn't do any good. The 21-inch thermite fire bombs worked so very well.

Up in the air, the blue flames of St. Elmo's fire, the static electricity phenomenon, danced and wiggled along the edges of his wings like the feathery cloaks of angels, he always thought, angels flying along with him. He loved the St. Elmo's colors and how it looked spinning in the edges of his propellers.

"The flag?" Charlie asked, so detached now that his friend felt like he was playing alone, though it wasn't that obvious to anyone how far Charlie was gone from the present moment. The flashbacks were contained in their unique, concentrated high-explosive bursts of visual event and feeling and fear and elation. They existed in that odd brain function where entire dramas could be reproduced in a totally clear, non-verbal re-enactment and all in a few seconds. A person who knew no words still had memory. The words only slowed it down. As it was, Charlie disappeared for a second, but was gone hours in his own mind. "Front, I guess."

Charlie had felt the heat from the burning city in the air where he flew. That much rising flame and temperature altered the way his plane handled, as it did the bombers that continued to come. He heard them talking about it on their radios, warning the trailing crews that they would be thrown upward by the heat.

The sky was scarlet and white like sunset. He was engulfed in colors and warmth. He flew above the flames and the blast of heated updraft in silence, deaf to everything except the brilliance of color below and around him. It was one of the most visually magnificent moments in his life, one of the most exalted and spiritual that notorious day, that evening, up in the air, alone, with God, somehow even with the violent incongruity of what was being done below, with God, it seemed. How else could he become a part of such wonder, rarity, such unearthly, heavenly beauty.

"I love this game," Paul said. He had just landed a ball on a green which had been trimmed as short and smooth as a GI's haircut.

The Spitfires had escorted the Lancasters and the Flying Fortresses as far as the Zuider Zee, where the Mustangs with their long range and high speed took over. The big planes got over the city and were caught in the intensity of the heated updrafts. The fresh air was sucked in from all sides from just beyond the burning mass where the flames were beginning to ignite, sucked toward the center of the city with greater force than normal winds, and all of that sparkling inferno shot upward toward Charlie and the planes.

He had seen the usual uprooted trees, giant trunks and stumps full of roots and clotted dirt that weighed tons tossed on top of each other or into roads and cultivated fields, blown loose as easily as a flipped Tiddly-Wink. He saw buildings returned to individual bricks and blocks, returned to dust, and vehicles in more parts than as they'd begun, all he'd seen before.

But then he saw something new. People or bodies or what was left of bodies, rose out of the city as if they, or the parts that they once were, were ascending to heaven. Hands, arms, whole bodies and what he thought were people still alive or just then in that very instant, dying, swirled upward from below him through the heated air, as if all of them and everything beneath were sucked skyward by the flaming, heated tornado, yet no tornado swirled, just the mirage and boiling confluence of exploded life below.

The explosions and superheated air from the flames of the burning city was sending the people and the details of their lives, their clothes, their papers, their hats and shoes and pets and hair and even faces, faces detached from heads and skulls, just the faces, he remembered, floating upward toward him and all around him, their eyes still open or their mouths in mid-sentence, sometimes, or open in horror, their lips peeled back in unfunny grins and yet some of them so lovely it had to be that they never knew they were dying, that they were being killed.

Another two-some had gained on them and Paul waved them past.

"My man here isn't fully awake this morning."

"How're you, Charlie?"

"Just fine."

Everyone knew almost everyone in a small town, just like in a platoon or company that had been together a long time. Paul tipped his hand and elbow toward his mouth and nodded toward his partner.

"That elbow bending'll catch up with you," he said.

Charlie flew through a smoke bank and came into a clearing where below him he saw nothing moving at first. Then, at a distance, he noticed a figure in motion in a way he could not understand, like a big man lumbering on all fours but with his head up in the air. He flew closer and saw it was a llama. He looked around further and realized that they had bombed the zoo, and the animals that were not dead or crippled trotted and bounded and walked as dazed as the people who had decided to come out of or been driven from their cellars.

He circled back toward the llama and saw that it had stopped right in front of a group of people who could have been, he thought, a family, the way they clung together. The llama and the people stood in the street looking at each other and then walked past one another as casually and routinely as if people passed llamas all day long in the streets. They walked past without looking back, without concern, neither animal nor human worried, at that time, about the other.

"You're drinking too much," Paul said.

The two-some played through and Charlie and Paul waited in their cart. Paul handed him a toothpick and they cleaned the spaces between their front and side teeth as they watched the two men drive with powerful and well taught swings, the balls soaring off the tees and into the air, precision instruments and expensively produced.

"Look there at that cart coming fast this way," Paul said. "They let anybody play these days. Some teenager, I guess."

Below him, the family in the street and the llama suddenly

moved backwards, as if they were sliding, but still standing, as if everything around them was suddenly moving backwards, everything but him and his plane which flew above it all, bucking and dropping and rising in the currents and updrafts, but still moving forward. Then, not in the kind of instant that a detonation occurs, but so very quickly as to startle him even more, the people and the animal disappeared into the firestorm that had caught up with them, pulling every living thing not below ground and every piece of timber and debris into it, the whole world below him sucked backwards and then upward, like earlier, toward his plane. All of them, the family and the llama and the entire human and animal and insect life on the street below him, began to burn and rise toward him like only holographic images now, not really there, just their imprint in the air, in all the glorious colors that life burns as it melts away.

CHAPTER 24

In the far room where the breading machines shook like the unbalanced tires of a car, Byrum saw Ellie in a wheelbarrow. She had leaned the handles down to the floor so that the other end, with the single wheel on it, was up in the air, and the barrow part, shaped like a seat with a sloping back, like a recliner now, was just at the right height for her to sit.

"I've been looking for you," Byrum said. "I've been running around so much I about got lost this morning doing everything for everybody."

"You know what," Ellie said.

"And see that man over there."

"Yes. I see him."

"That man is Tight Pants Tony. He never talks."

She raised her face toward Byrum. She pressed her forehead against his arm, which was braced on his knee as he bent down to talk to her.

"You're my buddy, you know," she said.

Tight Pants Tony got off the forklift and started toward Byrum, who looked at Ellie and then at Tight Pants and immediately apologized for whatever it was that was wrong.

"I was just standing here," he began. Tight Pants Tony reached behind himself like he was going to pull a gun from his waistband, but brought forth, instead, his wallet. It took a moment for him to work his hand into the tight pocket opening and then to squeeze the wallet up and out. Byrum backed away.

"Mr. Tony, do you know Ellie?"

Once he had the billfold, he removed two dollars and handed then to Byrum and returned to his forklift.

"He sometimes gives me money," he said.

"This is not a healthy place to work," Ellie said.

"I have more money."

"You could work somewhere else," she said. "I'm going to get you a job at a better place. You wanted to be a cook? We should try that. Almost anywhere is better than here. I like you too much. You could do fine anywhere."

"I can get some Lance crackers with this money."

"I've got so many things I need to do," she said. "So much I want to say. To so many people."

"You could talk what you want to say into your tape recorder," he said. "I'll give it you, and you keep it until break time. You want me to get another job?"

"I will talk into it. That's a good start. That'll help me organize everything."

"You can tell the story of your life like I'm doing. Only I can't stick around to hear it because Mr. Russell told me I got to clean up near the freezer where it's got slick. Do you want me to do something else?"

She took the recorder. Byrum's face was bright. He had the same cheerful look and yet in a way that was new to her, she saw something that touched her, saw what she thought was an almost apologetic self-awareness, something that told her he was aware how odd and limited he was, aware of it even as he was pleasantly and happily talking with her, that he knew that she knew he was different and that there was a divide between them that would always be there.

She tucked the recorder into her coat pocket. She noticed Gwen had moved to another machine and had hoisted a bag full of what looked like crumbs. She watched her friend heft the bag into the air and empty the contents into the blend. She kept one hand squeezed around the mouth of the bag to keep the crumbs from flowing too fast. She concentrated on the task for more than a minute before she noticed Ellie was observing.

"Breading," she yelled. "Or something like it."

Ellie nodded.

"Who knows what it really is."

Ellie shrugged her shoulders and turned her palms up, as if to answer, right, who knows? The truth was that everything was so loud she'd not even heard what her friend had said.

Becky tapped Ellie out of her reverie.

"You shouldn't be sitting down. I thought you were working with the girls. Are you ready to try another department?"

In the center room was a rack of floor scrapers, some resembling rusty, long-handled sand trap rakes and some similar to ancient golf clubs, like mashie niblicks. They hung behind the fryer. The implements were for scraping up pieces of burned chicken fat and skin that had spit from the grease and landed sizzling onto the concrete floor where they cooled and in doing so adhered to the chipped and porous surface.

"I need some time off this afternoon," Jay said, intent on not mentioning the job he wanted to apply for at the L'eggs factory.

"We don't have time for time off," Buck said.

Jessie leaned around one of the women who was shielding her and tried to catch Buck Ellis' eye. He noticed her but before she could indicate anything, he looked away.

"Well, I got to have time off."

"No time off."

In the other room, Ellie rose up from the wheelbarrow. When she took her weight off, it tipped back onto the front wheel and bounced. The grip end of one of the handles, in moving upward from where it touched the floor, caught the hem of Becky's long skirt and lifted it and scratched her leg and remained under her skirt so that when she tried to step away, the wheelbarrow moved sideways with her.

"How do I get out of here?" Ellie asked, looking the wrong way and starting off in that direction, which would have led her to the dead end part of the building opposite from the entrance.

"Get out?"

"I can't work here."

"You're leaving?"

"Just show me how to get to the front door."

"It'll get better. Try it a few more days."

"No."

Byrum came through a doorway empty-handed and Becky motioned him over.

"Are you busy right now?"

"Yes ma'am, I'm always busy."

"Walk this girl out of here and to the front door, please."

They walked in the trim room, in the far left end of the building. The only room further in that direction was the freezer with the wide plastic curtains.

"We go this way to get out," he said.

"I was supposed to meet my dad here," she said.

They went toward the fry room where Jay leaned under the unit to make one last check on the new connectors. He ran his hand around and over the joints, like a magician waving around a trick item to show there was nothing there.

"It's still leaking," Jay said.

"Where?"

"At the joint I spliced."

"Show me."

At 8:31 A.M. the hose blew apart.

It broke loose at one of the two joints he had spliced together trying to shorten the hose that had been sent much too long. It kicked backwards under 1,500 pounds of pressure. It sprayed Jay's fingers and arm and then it sprayed in all directions. A piece of the brass connector remained clamped into the loose hose and acted like a nozzle. The oil hit the air in a pressurized mist, finer and a hundred times harder than the mist out of an aerosol can.

"God-almighty," was all Buck was able to say before the hose, lodged in one spot against the metal corner of the fryer's leg like a cobra raised up and hissing, sprayed the oil directly into the gas burner's open flame.

The mist ignited. The hose then sprayed oily fire, like a flame thrower. It shot the incendiary fifty feet across the room igniting everything it hit and coating it like napalm, like fine droplets of napalm that adhered to walls, metal or people, and then set them on fire.

The burning oil coated the skin and surface of everything. Even if that surface would not normally burn, like the surface of metal, or ceramic, or concrete, it flamed up like dry charcoal in a grill sprayed with lighter fluid.

"Lookout," Buck said at the same time that the droplets ignited his eyebrows and eyelashes, the hair that stuck out underneath the cap on his head, and then his skin.

In the six seconds since the hose detached, Buck was on fire and Jay's arm and hand, already coated, burst into flame. The women's aprons, hanging below the level of the bottom of the vat where all the burners had ignited the spray like not just one flame thrower, but a series of them, caught fire.

The two men fell backwards to get out of the way and the women, almost as a group tied together not by apron strings but by fear, ran to their left, toward the trim room.

In ten seconds, the remaining section of coupler on the repaired hose came loose. Oil poured out now in a stream so powerful it would have knocked a person off balance just on its own, without needing to be aflame. A fireball in no defined shape, but as large as the entire group of women who now ran from it, formed in the air like a monster, as the air itself, now filled with oil droplets and mist, began to burn.

"Get outside," Lois said to her daughter. "Run outside."

"Where's the door?"

The air itself was on fire. Yellow and brown fumes outlined the burning ghostly shape. The flames and oil and the wavering colors moved across the room, through the air, chasing the women.

In fifteen seconds from when the hose first separated, the cloud of smoke and fumes had enveloped the people closest to it, and in another second or two, had the entire group inside it, covering them from their shoulders up so that their bodies and blue aprons, burning slowly and in conventional yellow and reddish flame, ran below the cloud like headless people, like a group that had had its head not in the clouds, but sliced off so quickly their bodies were still in motion in the direction they had been at the time the slice had been made.

Buck ran directly into a wall and bounced onto his back. He covered his face and head with his hands almost the same way Byrum had when he'd run from him earlier that day, except Buck's hands were also on fire. The women in this group saw none of this and continued running to their left. They bounced off machines and boxes and into a wall but stayed together.

Another group of women had been working to the right of where the fire began. They ran toward the other side of the room, where there was a hallway which led to an exterior door.

"What are they laughing at in there," someone asked Antonio, who had stopped worked to listen to the sounds coming from the other room.

"Doesn't sound like laughing."

The flames over the broiler burned into the ceiling through the cardboard tile and into the mechanical space above it. Electric wires sparked and spit and then, before anyone in the rest of the building knew what was happening, lights in a couple of the rooms went out. There were no windows and no battery operated illuminated signs above any of the doors. Nearly complete darkness descended on everyone in those rooms so fast that the blink of an eye reopened into night.

In the thirty seconds since the fire began, Ellie and Byrum neared the doorway leading into the processing room. They saw the women coming toward them, and at the same time that they saw that, the room went dark so that the only thing they could make out from then on was what was illuminated by the oil and air burning from that room.

Ellie grabbed Byrum's arm.

People ran from all over toward them and the front entrance. As they got closer they realized the processing room was where the fire was. It was through that room they had to pass to get out the double front doors.

"The whole place is on fire," a man near the storage room said to another man. "That's what it sounds like in there. We better go see."

"It can't be," the other man said. "Brick and block can't burn. Must just be that one fryer unit again."

"We can put that out. Grab that extinguisher."

In the break room, the Lance man heard the noise and noticed the electricity blinking at the machine next to the one he was packing. He heard the safety switch click as the motor, having shut on and off too abruptly, stopped and waited. It was so quiet in there in that one moment he could even hear the timer on the reset switch ticking. Then he heard the word, fire, and saw the yellowish smoke coming from the doorway.

"We can get out the exit in the break room," someone calmly said. "Let's think a moment and figure this out. Don't panic."

In the annex across the street, George's computer blinked and went out. Becky pointed across the road.

"They're calling you, or calling for something," she said and pointed out a window to a couple of employees who fell out the front door and onto the sidewalk just as he looked out the window.

"Fire," one of them said quietly, not like a trained rescue person conveying the fact efficiently, but like a zombie. "Fire."

George went inside and saw how thick the smoke was and ran back to the front of the building and picked up a telephone. The line was dead.

In the trim room, Ellie held Byrum's arm and followed the women into the break room where the lights were still on, but flickering like staggered Christmas tree lights.

Evelyn, who had just a few weeks earlier used the exit door in that room to carry a box of filets outside, grabbed the handle. She twisted the knob and then shoved against the door and mashed the panic bar that usually didn't need any force at all.

"It won't open."

Someone else tried.

"It's locked."

Two women and the Lance man kicked the door and a group broke off from this original cluster of workers and ran out of the break room.

The smoke from the fryer units had filled the room so that it was almost entirely dark, even with the flames and the light coming from the hall near the break room. As they looked briefly in that direction, Jay ran full speed out of the smoke and into their group like a football player, with his head down and his arms in front of him, against his chest, as if clutching a football, except he was clutching his own arms, one of which had the skin hanging off. He knew something was there and he could feel it but not see it. He thought it was grease dripping from his forearm, not his skin dripping off.

"The cooler," someone said, and all of them walked in that direction, feeling the way inside by the plastic curtains.

Less than a minute and a half since the fire had started, George drove his car four blocks to the fire station. There were two full time fire-fighters there, and they sounded the alarm, a siren located on top of the fire station, and paged their volunteers, all 28 of them.

CHAPTER 25

"There's the siren, too," Paul said as he and Charlie tried to finish their game. "I know the A-bomb's been dropped now. See? I was right."

Charlie was thirsty and his mouth felt as dry as a sand trap. He heard sirens, too, but they were the real thing, the air raid sirens from the war. They sounded in his ears just as eerily and wavering as they had when he flew above them.

"Now there's that's speeding cart again. We got to turn that person in to the committee," Paul said, and noticed his friend was now more pale than earlier in the morning.

The bombing, Charlie later learned, had been done during the Carnival performances, something that the town did every year on Ash Wednesday.

Charlie remembered how he circled carelessly and dangerously above the city during the time between the first wave of bombers and when the second would come. If he was below them then, he would likely be hit by his forces' own bombs on the way down. He was up there too long, and he was running low enough on his fuel that he might not make it back if he didn't soon leave.

"What cart?"

He saw a group of brightly decorated horses huddled against a building. He saw a big sign on the ground that said Circus Sarassani. In that lull that only he knew was a lull, and not the population, not the people below who assumed, prayed and hoped was not a lull but the end of the bombing, he saw people running out of cellars and tunnels. He saw a huge glass-roofed courtyard that had remained intact, though everything around it was hit and pieces of debris were on top of it and he could see that its supports around the perimeter were damaged.

He watched a group of girls, wearing costumes and ribbons, run from a building and into the courtyard which they crossed and he saw them through the smoky glass like viewing a tableau in motion on a stage, the girls and their bright clothes running this way and that, all as a pack, as one, trying to get the gates open to get out, and then, still circling above, he saw the glass roof crash down on them.

For just a moment, as the flames reflected in the glass and the bright clothes all mixed together, it was like looking in a dazzling kaleidoscope and it mesmerized him so he wanted to look through it forever, watching the colors of the girls and their clothes and the flames and the glass combining and tumbling in such a display it was yet another stunning moment, unlike any piece of art or act of nature with which he was familiar, something so brilliant he found himself slowly falling toward it, guiding his plane downward, as if he wanted to be a part of it.

"Mr. Russell," the black man hurtling toward them in the cart called.

"Is he calling you?" Paul asked.

"Mr. Russell. Yo factory be on fire."

"What'd he say?" Charlie asked, the man still too far away to be clearly heard and he, himself, distant and lost and confused.

"It's Alfred. Slow down, Alfred, we can't hear you."

"I say," he told them as he braked beside their cart. "Yo plant is burning. They's people inside. Come on. Quick."

Five minutes from the fire, in Dobbins Heights, in a two-bay garage with brightly painted automatic roll-up doors, a tax-supported set of fire trucks sat already warmed by the sun, their engines ready to start, their tires polished wet-black, their windshields clean and their hoses dry and folded as neatly as socks in a military dresser drawer awaiting inspection.

"Sounds big," Arthur 'Lumbee' Farver said to another man who had driven quickly to the station when they heard the siren. "Did you have your scanner on?"

"Yeah."

"Where is it?" Farver asked.

"In Hamlet."

"I can tell that from the siren."

"Maybe it's nothing."

"You know it's not nothing."

"Yeah," he answered, still evading the answer.

"Turn that thing on. Why'd you turn it off?"

"Because it's the chicken plant on fire."

Not only did Farver's niece Lois work there, but so did the man she almost married, who was not only the father of her child, but was his friend, as well.

"They been on fire before. It's usually the grease."

"Yeah, I know," he said, turning up the scanner and listening as departments from nearby towns were called. "Sounds like more than that this time."

Four more men parked on the side of the station and put on their suits and boots and stood beside the first two men, who were already dressed.

"Let's go," one of them said.

"They hadn't called us yet," Farver said.

"What? That doesn't make sense. They're calling every other department from farther away than us."

"You want to go on over?" one of them asked. "I mean, drive on over by yourself. To check on Lois?"

"I'll wait. Let's just be ready. They'll be calling if it's as bad as it might be."

"We are the closest back-up station," one of the men said.

"I'll wait. Let's get the masks and apparatuses ready."

"They got to call us. We're the closest."

"Let's be ready."

The men checked on the breathing and protection devices and then, already in the boots and long coats and helmets, leaned against the front of the truck and listened to the intermittent squawk of clipped rescue language over the radio. The front doors to the station were raised. Soon a car pulled up.

"Move out, man," the young fellow in the car yelled. "There's people all trapped inside the chicken plant. I'm going over there now."

The men looked at him but no one said anything or even conveyed an expression of interest. In a few seconds, he drove off, and then the firefighters, now silent, didn't even look at one another.

They could feel the heroic and courageous reserve building up inside of them that would be needed once they got there, the kind of action and speed and coordination that would be necessary. They let it build like soldiers ready to go over the top. The truck engines were now idling, and the pumps, which ran off the main engines from a power take-off connection, were self-priming and would take only a few seconds to provide all the water pressure necessary. The men themselves were ready to go, motivated by not only the knowledge that so many of their friends worked there, but by the unspoken understanding that they would have to prove themselves to their white counterparts.

At the plant, a group of workers further from where the fire began ran toward one of the loading docks. They found it blocked by the tractor and trailer that had been there since early that morning. The driver in the cab remained asleep.

Outside the building, the fire trucks arrived and were directed to front, back and sides of the building and hooked to the hydrants. The fire itself was not yet visible outside the structure, but yellow and gray and black smoke seeped from cracks where the walls met the roof. In some places what emitted was one color, depending on what burned close by. In others, they combined so that the effect was something like banana fudge ripple in color, only melted and steamy.

Jay's father stopped his pickup. The dash-mounted red lights rotated and then stopped as the engine died. He ran toward the building carrying his boots in one hand, which he switched to the other as he put on his coat. His helmet was loose and the straps slapped his neck as he got into his gear without slowing down.

The women who'd been working on the right side of the room and were now in the hallway pounded on the door, which, unknown to them until this moment, had been one of the exits locked a month earlier. They looked at the smoky inferno, not seeing flames from where they were, only a dark, concentrated billowing mass obscuring everything as it moved toward them.

From out of the boiling oil, spheres of fire bounced toward them, round, crimson-colored contractions of gas and flame that were the size of beach balls. They launched upward from the fryer unit, gathering along the surface of the cooking oil and forming a spinning, round shape. They rose and actually hurtled toward them, as if someone in that now totally dark room was throwing them, one after another.

Meanwhile, around back, the driver asleep in the cab under the influence of twice the dosage of sleeping pills he normally took to unwind from the amphetamines he took to get the loads to where he needed to in time, began to think that the sirens he'd heard at such a distance were actually right there beside him and the bumping and knocking and calling he had been hearing was not simply the sound of boxes being loaded into the trailer but was something else. At about the time he realized that, someone jerked open his door.

"Move the damn truck. People are trapped."

"Huh?"

"The damn building's on fire."

He pulled the truck forward. A mass of people tumbled from the building to the pavement. They fell like giant Snickers' bars tossed onto the ground. The people were that black, that coated in grime and soot, that uniform and inhuman looking, falling like burnt, charcoal logs.

Ellie and Byrum, still holding each other, were in the break room behind Antonio and a few women. The people in front of them kicked the door. The lights blinked a few more times and then the room went black. An eerie, brownish-yellow glow from the processing room was now the only light they had, and in just a few seconds the smoke became so thick that even that faint glow, about as bright as a four-watt night-light would be in a completely darkened house, was extinguished. The darkness was darker than they had ever seen, as dark as the inside of a casket buried in the ground, a kind of heavy blackness that was tangible, as if it, itself, had to be pushed through, as the smoke became so heavy it made darkness solid.

The first firemen, now eight minutes into the fire, entered the front door, the only way they could find into the building. The heat and smoke were so intense they reversed almost right away, holding the shoulders of the man in front of them. They walked backwards, shining their lights into the building on their way out, but seeing nothing. The front man held a rope. His intention had been to attach it as far inside as he could get so that they could crawl holding to it and find their way out once they were confused or overcome or turned around.

On the sidewalk, three bodies were already out of the building. They were black in color, like the ones out back, and from a distance it wasn't possible to determine their race.

Fourteen people were in the freezer, separated from the group that remained in the break room. The plastic curtains, always dim and distorted like scratched and degraded Plexiglas on the clearest of days, were covered with soot and deformed by the heat, curling up like cheap plastic containers inside a microwave, folding inward like a wide open palm closing into a fist.

The air was cold as usual, but there wasn't much of it, as the oxygen was used up by the hyperventilating state of everyone in there, as well as the flames, which sucked the air from everywhere inside the building to feed the fire.

Above the fryer, which now blazed as if it contained not soybean oil, but kerosene, an extinguishing system full of soda and powder, similar to what was installed in almost all restaurants over the deep fat cookers, was singed and so hot skin would have melted into it had anyone tried to release, by hand, the emergency lever that should have set the system into motion. The unit, which had been installed under direct state and local inspectors' orders back in 1983 when the first fire had been investigated, failed.

In a cheap, metal addition near the compactor, people had run not expecting a way out, because there were no doors out of it, but because in running they had ended up here merely by escaping the flames and fireballs that chased them from behind until there was nowhere to go but there.

They clawed at the thin panels, which buckled but would not bend enough to squeeze through to the outside. Smoke filled this room and the harder they kicked, the harder they breathed, and the harder they breathed, the faster they declined in the ability to think or function anyway at all, as the smoke and toxic fumes replaced the oxygen not only in the room, but in their lungs.

"I'm going in," Jay's father said as he stood in the entrance to the plant, leaning away from the door as smoke and fumes poured out one of the few openings to the outside.

From all around the building the firemen began to locate the people inside, and understood, finally, that they were clumped against the doors and as trapped from coming out as they, themselves, were from going in.

"Break open the walls and every door you see."

"Where?"

"Anywhere. Take a damn truck and ram it into a wall. Do something. Do anything."

At the compactor, in the narrow space where it did not reach the top of the loading dock, two people were wedged. Their heads and necks were outside the building, but the rest of their bodies were inside. All around them through the opening above the compactor, smoke poured out like it had the front door. The two people looked as if they were stuck in the top of a chimney above a blazing fireplace.

Suddenly the smoke coming out lessened and almost stopped for an instant before it began once more. Behind these people, the roof above the fryer had finally burned through to the air, opened up toward the sky, and the smoke that filled the building tightly with nowhere to go but within, rushed upward through the hole. The firemen outside now knew from that where the origin and worst place was, and they sent people up to chop open the space where the flames roared upward, and to contain the burn on the roof itself to that one spot, if possible.

Behind the plant, coming from the old Seaboard station, a man who looked like a hobo, but one who had dressed as well as he could for the day, as if he'd cleaned himself up to look for work in the new town he had arrived at by boxcar, as if he'd washed his clothes by taking a shower in them and then dried out by walking in the sun, ambled toward the chicken plant.

The man had left where he'd stayed the night and found a set of tracks and started west on them. A person anywhere near Hamlet could find the town by walking the rails. All he would have had to do was determine whether he was east of the town, for instance, and then walk west, or if he was in South Carolina, walk north. Every track in that area eventually entered the town and the yards and the station, which itself was within sight of Capital Food Products.

A heavy growth of trees and plants, some of them thirty feet tall on trunks or stalks no more than two inches in diameter, obscured most of the building from the man's vision until he got close enough to see that the fire trucks were there and that the static and speaker-modulated talking he'd heard was from them and the police and rescue vehicles.

He tripped on a Cheerwine bottle and kicked up some loose crushed stone as he regained his balance, looking like a staggering drunk about to fall on his face. The rails on either side of him were recently laid and all the crossties were bedded solidly, and the tracks, over which he now stepped, were shiny from the amount of freight traffic they handled day in and out.

"Hello, Bob," one of the policeman said when he recognized the man. "Don't get too close."

The man was Ellie's father. He was trying, in his own way, to honor what he'd said to his daughter. He'd recovered from the drinking he and Robbie had done the previous night, and had arrived there to apply, as he'd said he would, for a job. He had not been able to find his friend so his ride to the job failed. His brain, about as clear and light as a bale of wet cotton, had miraculously retained the promise he'd made.

CHAPTER 26

Jay had stepped over Buck when he'd found the group of women fleeing that room. Buck's face was not burning by that time. His skin no longer hurt. The conflict between his desire for oxygen and the presence of soot and carbon monoxide left him weak and barely conscious. He was covered in debris and ash. He was flat on the floor. The effort to breathe, to draw in anything but air as abrasive as a sandstorm, cancelled out the pain from the burn. All he wanted, all he knew, was to fill his lungs with air. He'd have given everything he owned, everything he would ever own, everything he would ever be able to do, for oxygen.

If Buck had been hung, for instance, lynched, something he'd threatened to do to people many times before this day, his dying would have been different from what he now struggled against, though it, too, would have involved the blood and the brain and the air. Cerebral oximia, or the lack of blood to the brain, was what killed in hanging, because any ligature around the neck, applied even modestly tight, closed the vessels which carried the oxygenated blood up there, and it was that, not the closure of the throat and the air passages there, which caused death by hanging.

Buck's dying was slower than hanging.

Because of the damage to his face and the increasing amount of smoke he was inhaling, and his fear and panic, the sound of the words were inhuman, more like animal sounds, more like he'd heard from raccoons he'd shot but hadn't quickly died, their dark, bandit eyes so deeply amber in their centers, their onyx claws—sharp enough to rake open the bellies of half a dozen black-and-tan hounds—now turned under and scraping their own stomachs raw of that lush Davey Crockett coonskin cap fur.

He sounded like one of them.

He made the same noise that gut-shot and fallen deer made as he stood over them before reaching down and slicing their throats. At that point the noises they made incorporated the sound of liquid, bubbles coming out the mouth in pale reds and bursting ever so gently into the air just beyond the animal's lips like pink champagne.

If Buck had been surprised from the rear and strangled by some angry human he had degraded some time in his life, he might have died faster and easier. It only took eleven pounds of pressure to close off the carotid artery, only four pounds of pressure to shut down the jugular vein, which was the one that brought the blood back to the heart, but that was not happening to him at the moment, which was not good, because his dying was slower, much slower than strangulation. Worse.

He got partially onto his hands and knees but no further, rocking backward like an old bear whose back legs had been shot out from under him.

If his airway had been closed, or crushed, rather than fighting for some air that had less oxygen than smoke as he did now, he would have made a funny face. His tongue would be protruding and his jaw would have moved upward, making him look even uglier than he had in better times, only minutes earlier. Instead, because of the burns on his cheeks, lips and eyelids, and the now liquid skin, he looked more like a freshly skinned rabbit.

The human head weighed ten to twelve pounds, except for Buck's, which weighed more. It slumped forward now, as he fought to stay on his hands and knees, leaning down like a cow's toward the ground. His face became congested, enlarged beyond its normally angry, swollen look. What remained of his skin that wasn't pink was reddish and blue under the coating of soot and smoke and burned meat, and around his neck, which hadn't been in flames, small, flat spots called petechiae appeared, so that he looked a little flea bitten.

He fell onto the greasy spot where Cecelia had slipped earlier in the morning, and where a piece of chicken skin had been stepped on so often it was mashed into the concrete like a possum in the highway that had been run over a thousand times. His cheek lay against the skin.

Dying quickly usually involved the interference of the lungs or heart and some sort of asphyxia, and most people became cyanotic, though before that, there could be a progression of drowsiness, delirium and then, if the person was lucky, a coma.

Buck was not that lucky.

It took only four parts per thousand of carbon monoxide to kill a person, but that took an hour, and when a person died that way, his skin turned red or pink first, the color of cherry Popsicles or peach snow cones, and then, as time went on, more blackish. Dying in the chicken plant on the floor under blankets of smoke, soot, gasses and toxic particles, not to mention heat and flames hurtling above in the room like meteors flashing by in the nighttime sky, was the ugliest sight Buck Ellis had ever presented to the world.

He tried to yell but all the words were coming out now like grunts, like hog sounds.

After death by carbon monoxide, convulsions followed. Buck motivated across the room like he was break dancing, like he was some street dude with a boom box who had hit the sidewalk in a cool move and was now on his side, then on his back, then on his side again, break dancing and sliding and jerking around in circles and across the floor. Technically, the movements were not Buck's attempt to finally learn to dance, or some secret desire to be an African American, even though he was now that color, from head to foot, inside his mouth and nostrils and even under his fingernails, but the movements were because brain damage was occurring.

The problem with rescuing someone from a carbon monoxide death, with saving them from actual physical death, was that the brain damage continued for weeks, and the pyramid cells in the hypo-campus portion of the brain continued to die for those days or weeks that followed. If Buck were to live, he would eventually have little more to offer the world than one of the cucumbers he grew in his garden.

Alone in the middle of the processing room, Buck break-danced across the floor, first in one direction and then another, jerking inward and then opening up quickly like a really cool move, again and again. His legs kicked like he was running on his side, like he was trying to spin and run around in circles while he lay there, and he threw his head back and forth and clutched his arms to his chest as if he was hugging someone only to throw them open again.

He skidded and bounced along the floor until he rolled over a pair of boots that someone had leaped out of when running away. He convulsed a few more times and these last violent floor-bound leaps threw him against the legs of the women trapped against a locked door.

Then, as if he were trying to ascend, as if his soul was trying to get out of his doomed and sinful body and move up to heaven, but failing, he rose off the floor and up into the air and into the crowd of women, who screamed even louder in the dark as the massive weight of Buck Ellis hovered over them and then fell back to the slab, the same piece of perfect concrete work that years earlier men had labored to lay on the ground so that for as long as possible and for all the good that could come of it, people would be gathered upon it to earn a way to live and survive.

None of the rooms had electricity. The fire department shut off all power to the plant, and closed the outside valves to the natural gas lines. When that was done, the flames in the burners went out, and at nearly the same time, the hydraulic pumps ceased, and no new accelerant was added to the oil-laden air.

Across the top of the vats flames already lively skimmed along as usual and picked up the surface of the superheated cooking oil and sent it around the building in the nightmarish balls of soybean napalm that continued to float from room to room, carried along by the heated air and the rush of diminishing oxygen that was pulled like wind through the building.

Outside, Charlie Russell showed up dressed in his golf yellows. He was allowed through the cordons and he found George standing with his arms crossed, on the other side of Bridges Street, at the front door of the administrative annex.

"What happened?"

"I think it was that leaking line," he said and then both men looked at each other and knew they could and would say no more about it. It was not the passing of familial connection that occurred, but the knowledge of law and liability that moved between the two men, not the father saying to the son that we, you and I, have failed, that from this day on nothing will be the same. The three bodies in front of them on the sidewalk and the others that fell like smoked versions of the Three Stooges tumbling in a mass pratfall on top of each other as a false wall gives way, were tragic results of events and decisions they knew too well, and at the same time, knew nothing about at all.

If this were a circus act, it might have been funny to see the bodies and live wiggling figures come out like that, a one time humorous, knee-slapping sight now as terrifying to see as a pile of death camp corpses tossed out the back door of the furnace, as sad and hideous to see as Rwandan human tragedies left on the side of the road, bodies in motion and then still. The two men, father and son, stopped talking, stared at each other, closed their lips, set their jaws, blinked and then looked around at their business, now in flames.

Charlie and his son watched a couple of firefighters hacking at one of his locked exits with pointed steel bars as long as spears. He watched them ram the flattened, pry bar ends against the door jam. They pried and pulled and stabbed against the block and metal. Pieces of masonry spit off the walls as the pressed steel jams twisted and the door popped open like the lid of a jack-in-the-box.

Only one person was behind this latest door that had been pried open. It was Cecelia, her red hair mostly gone and her skull singed with stipples of pink and yellow dust caught in the few strands that remained, her eyes sooty beneath the sockets, her lips oddly blue against a lemon chiffon-pie colored skin, the result of some toxic burst into her face. Her ears were long, like a cocker spaniel's, and her nose flattened and small like a gray button.

"I don't know what to do," George said.

Smoke, like the big marking flares had produced, poured out of the building.

"I can't believe this," Charlie said.

"What are we going to do?"

They called over to the chief and asked him but he had no answers.

The smoke swirled and made a pattern, like the swirl of different colors and flavors in a chocolate sundae.

The air in the lower half of the door just forced open sucked inward and met the heated higher air rushing out so that as Cecelia fell through the sudden opening, she twirled, like she was dancing again, only more gracefully in death than before.

"Who's that?"

"I don't know."

"Looks worse than the ones before."

In the main freezer people were alive, though some of them were in the last minutes of being in that condition. They huddled and waited to be rescued. They made noises. They buried their faces into one another. They clung. They prayed.

Even with the power off, even with flames and heat all around the cold space, the room-sized unit would hold things frozen for hours.

"I can't see," Carly whispered, and then said it louder as she panicked when her mother didn't answer.

It was darker there, too, than merely dark in the normal way the inside of a freezer would be. It was as dark as fear itself, as dark as if fear was a hand closing off the eyes, nose and mouth of everyone in there.

"Don't talk," Lois said. She had to speak loudly herself to be heard above the noise.

"Is Uncle Arthur coming?" Carly asked, remembering that he was a fireman.

"Yes. And soon. Don't talk."

The smoke seeped into the room. It hit the frigid air and dropped to the floor onto everyone who lay together, close at first, to keep warm, and then unable to move, incapacitated by their rapidly filling lungs.

"Honey," Lois said to her daughter in her lap. "Put this over your head." She repeated it so she could be heard and choked and coughed from the intake.

She pulled two boxes off the shelf, feeling for them first and locating two closest to them and then finding the flaps and dumping out the frozen breasts. "Slip this over your head. Breath inside it. Make a safe place in there where the bad air can't get you."

She put one over her own face and felt to see if her daughter had done it properly.

"Pull it down and keep that smoke out of your mouth," she said and buried herself into the box and leaned over on top of her daughter.

Ellie was in the room with all these people but heard nothing. The sounds they made were lost in all the other sounds around her, cracking sounds and sudden explosive bursts and groaning, not only of people but of wood and steel as it sagged, changed shape, twisted and popped loose from where it had been for decades. She did hear, though, the sound of her own heart and her own breathing, heard them distinctly the way laboratory subjects reported that once they were inside scientifically soundless rooms the sounds of their own bodies roared so loudly it scared them. She also heard Byrum.

She held his head and shoulders against her breast. His legs were drawn up and resting on the floor, and both her arms were around his back, squeezing him to her. He made the kind of sound she once heard when she and Ricky stopped to help someone in a car wreck, and were there before the rescue personnel. It was a distant, rhythmic wail that rose and fell with the expulsion of the trapped man's breath as he lay crushed in the car. It had seemed to be coming from somewhere deep within the man, not produced in the normal way by his vocal chords and throat, but from someplace deeper inside. Now Byrum made those same sounds.

He was back in the institution. It was so dark everybody was afraid. The sounds from the other people were new. The beds were all around him like radios, big radios making sounds he couldn't turn off and hated to hear. Nothing could stop the sounds. Nothing could stop what was happening to him.

A big fan was built into the ceiling above him, not the friendly kind like in stores and restaurants that turned slowly and clicked like a rocking chair going back and forth on a creaky porch floor, but a terrifying kind of fan, directly over his bed. He watched it at first and then tried not to see it. It had louvers that opened suddenly whenever the blades turned, and the blades started like a gunshot. He would be lying in bed and the fan would snap on and the louvers would open up above him and every little thing around him would begin to move, pieces of paper and dust off the floor and from under the beds with their high steel legs painted white but chipped and rusty and bad to run into with his bare feet and with his toes.

Everything moved when that big fan came on. It was so dark up in the fan, inside the blades. Then, in the night, it might shut off, and the slats would slam together like the way the men who worked there would come up behind him and slap their hands together and make him jump.

And another bad thing. It got hotter when the fan was on and all the hot and humid air from outside came inside until later in the night when it got cold and colder and no one had a sheet because it costs money to launder the top sheets so you can get along without them in the summer. What do you care anyway you're lucky we give you someplace to live and something to eat, don't complain.

Byrum tried to be still like Ellie told him to do.

That's the way it was in the freezer, dark and cold but the hot things were all up near his head and up at the ceiling and everyone was yelling to stay down and to stay still and not breathe but how could he not breathe? He tried it but he had to breathe and it made him cry. A grown man cried.

"I can't breathe."

He kicked forward, swimming through the bodies. He crawled. He bumped into the walls and the other people on the floor. He went the wrong way and ended up at the back wall, on top of everyone else who had pushed as far away from the smoke as they could get. He crawled the other direction. He made the eerie moaning noises and Ellie heard him and found what she thought was his shirt, moving away from her. She pulled him back. She kept her mouth shut, her lips pressed together, to keep out the smoke and said nothing, just held to his shirt and tried to roll him against her legs and back into her arms. She patted him and kept him as still as she could.

Bob McCorkle stumbled past the police, most of whom knew him, as he continued down the tracks and around the front of the building, past the railroad sidings that were rarely used now that everything moved by truck, and past the huge groups of air conditioning and compressor units.

All the oxygen in the vicinity, all the available air in the town of Hamlet, rushed toward the flames, drawn there in the same way that the people of the town now parked their vehicles and stood, shoulder to shoulder, hundreds and then thousands of them, the entire town, watching the spectacle, not laughing, not talking, just arms folded and touching each other in the mass, leaning against each other without knowing it, the crowd now as one, holding everyone within it up, and quiet, not a sound, not a word coming from all those people held back behind the police and fire lines.

McCorkle looked at the cars in the parking lot, now jammed with trucks and rescue vehicles in no order, every avenue and clear space back a hundred feet from the building clogged. He walked among the lots and around to the front on Bridges Street, looking for his daughter's car.

Jay's father started in again, but was held back. Smoke poured out of the hole chopped in the roof.

"I am going in," he said to the chief.

"We're about ready. Make sure you have plenty of air in the tanks."

"We're going to need more. More tanks, more people," he said to the chief.

"We might."

"Call in Dobbins. They're three minutes away."

"We don't need them. I don't want their help."

The chief organized the firefighters who were now showing up from further away, from Rockingham and beyond, from the stations he had requested, trucks and personnel from distant towns and rural areas all over the county.

Fire departments were prohibited from simply arriving at a disaster and had to be called in by the jurisdiction in charge. The chief knew that some of the outlying people and their equipment were also at the Hamlet station, manning it in case of some other fire or accident that might be called in. They would then take care of it while the Hamlet department was involved at Capital.

A group of men with brilliant hand-held lights and oxygen masks entered, moving along the rope that had been secured within, holding to it like people sliding their hands along a rope bridge as they crossed over a gorge, the firefighters even walking the same way, clumsy and uncertain, not knowing what it was they set their feet against or stepped on or over.

They found bodies. They found living people. They led them out. As they emerged, rescue personnel and medical workers who had driven a few blocks from the hospital took over. Large box fans as big as washing machines were in every doorway that could be opened, drawing out the smoke. Thick electrical cords ran from them to the generators built into the fire trucks.

McCorkle saw his daughter's car. He scanned the crowd and then walked around the entire building looking for her.

The break room was now solid with smoke and gasses and the people closest to the locked door that had been kicking against it were on the slab, not still, but not able to rise up, crawling sometimes, but not far, like puppies in a pile, like newborn kittens flopping over one another looking for mother.

The harder anyone tried to get out, the harder he or she breathed, and the more debris they took into their lungs. It was, for the worst of them, no easier to breathe than if they'd stuck their face into a sandbox and tried to suck in sand. They choked, they spit, their eyes ran, tear ducts abraded and raw.

Oxygen and what it had to do was complex but so perfectly organized within the body that just a few things wrong threw everything off. It was carried from the nostrils and mouth into the throat. Imagine how much it hurt to swallow and to cough when a person had a severely sore, raw throat. Double that discomfort, triple it, and with every attempt at breathing, the workers felt that. The less oxygen there was, the faster the organs and tissue declined, and the faster logic, clear thinking, coordination and strength failed.

The Lance man, now on the floor, wasn't dead, but was clinically experiencing what would be referred to on medical reports as severe pulmonary edema. His mouth was as frothy as if he'd stuffed 50 peanut butter crackers inside and then tried to chew and swallow them without opening his mouth or taking a drink of water. Particles bubbled out in the froth while he lay on the floor. Bits of tissue and spittle and sooty mucous that hadn't stuck to the membranes within his mouth, throat and lungs dribbled down his chin and onto his chest, something like the mass of chewed rancid peanuts that Buck had hawked out his truck window.

Suddenly the door gave way and people fell forward and into the arms of the rescue personnel who'd finally thought to ask for the keys and opened it after hearing the banging and searching for and locating yet another locked exit. Smoke poured out as well, and caused everybody outside to duck their heads to avoid it. Once low to the ground, they pulled the bodies out.

A backhoe that was at a nearby work site showed up. It was directed to the huge, green compactor. Above the metal rim at the top, in the narrow space near the building, a total of three people had managed to get their head and shoulders out of the building, into the air. When the backhoe pushed the compactor away from the building, they fell to the ground along with a few other workers who'd been mashing against it from the inside.

Ellie's father watched the people strike the ground, hitting it with the same boneless quality of drunks falling down flights of stairs. He picked up an oxygen mask from the ground around the back of the building near a pile of firefighter's gear. It had a single, green bottle attached to it. He put the mask over his head but backwards, so that the breather nose and eye shields were over the rear. He pulled it up and off. When he did, he tore the bottom of one of his ears. Blood trickled down his neck the way it had dozens of times from being in fights or scuffles and having his ears pulled or torn or twisted by angry men and women.

He properly put on the mask and at a spot on the building where the doors were open but very little smoke came out, he entered. He was at the far end from the fire, in an addition that was separated by a series of hallways, one of them the hallway where four people now lay against yet another locked door.

He wandered into the first hall, where he could see about as well as he might have in a night club with a pair of sunglasses on. He could see any bright shape or glow, but nothing unlit, nothing that wasn't illuminated by flame. He felt along the walls and the further he went, trailing his fingertips along the brick and tile interior, the hotter it got.

He tripped on bodies, which he knew the very instant his foot hit, were bodies. He quickly fell on top of them, into them, the same way he had fallen on top of drunks, the same kind of formless, pliant mass that was hard to get out of sober, much harder than that drunk, sinking into the limp bodies that offered no resistance off which to push. He struggled to get out of the pile, but it was like fleshy quicksand, like being in a bowl of stew. As soon as he found a body to push against, he sunk into it or it moved or rolled or gave way. He crawled forward, his hands in the people's faces, his knees on their stomachs and legs and backs, until he got past them and onto the concrete.

He walked again, bent over, one hand sliding against the wall, the other in front, feeling back and forth, searching for the doorway that would get him to the interior of the building. He had a sense of where his daughter was. He was being led through the maze of halls and rooms and dead ends and machinery by some sense he was not fully aware of but was real within him, heading right for Ellie.

He turned the corner and entered the processing room and was knocked off his feet by the heat and the smoke, which rushed toward him when he pulled back on the interior door that had partially closed. Still loaded with alcohol from the night before, and from the past twenty years, he, himself, was something like a walking incendiary device. The liquor oozed out his pores and the hotter he got, the more it oozed, as if he was a pig on a spit over an open fire being cooked but instead of fat and grease dripping from him, since there was little of that, the alcohol simmered out his skin, drawn out as if he was being rendered of it, as if he was distilling it himself, a sweat and corn liquor mix.

Then, crawling and delirious with the heat, and weak and suffocating from the empty canister that had been with the discarded mask, he burst into flame like a dog that had been soaked in kerosene and set alight by vandals. He rolled over near an unconscious Byrum.

Fifty feet away, in the freezer, Ellie held another person in her arms, still thinking it was Byrum, she herself now limp and collapsed onto that person, who was, himself, already dead. She was conscious, but too weak to move. She noticed that everything had become quiet, that there were no sounds at all deep within that thick-walled freezer, no talking, no crying, no praying, no scuffling or scratching or movement of any kind.

She began then, acutely alert within her mind, but with a torpid, exhausted shell of a body, to understand yet one more thing on that horrible day of revelations. She began to understand that she was dying, and that this was what it was like, the silence, the stillness, the fatigue so complete that she could do nothing to overcome it, could do nothing to roll away or run away or even wish away the sense of dying that she understood was now within her.

She was, though she couldn't know it then, at the very crossroads between life and death, at the station where she had a few minutes to try to go back, alone, it seemed to her by the depth of the silence and the stillness of everything that she should have been aware of. She was at the moment when belief could fail. She had that brief time to combine the words of belief with the effort to believe, the few minutes when she could give in and let go, or turn back. Ellie lay there, in that space, in that divide, in a deep, expectant quiet, and waited.

Not far away in a gritty, boiling battlefield of human obstacles, her father rolled one more time, a complete revolution of his body which carried him away from Byrum. As he did, an burst of fire retardant soda powder gushed down on top of him and Byrum like a avalanche of dry snow. The retardant system had sat intact for so many years that its sensors had gotten caked in grease and dirt and they had never, until that moment, received the signals of heat and smoke needed to release their load. When they did, it was as if a giant box of baking soda had been dumped onto the men, covering them in three inches of powder. Then, as suddenly it had begun, the soda stopped as the canisters mounted above the fryers emptied.

One of the men so important to Ellie lay fifty feet away from her, snuffed and dropped to the floor by every mistake, every error, every mean-spirited, misguided, desperate idea and bad call and haughty, prideful posture that had been set before him in his life, every thing that had gone wrong, had gone awry, every drink and drug that had coated him like a polymer, a man satin-varnished like a floor, laid down and walked on until his heart was wood, his mind a soak of gin and whiskey, given up on and given away by everyone except for Ellie, a man only a daughter could love.

Sirens continued.

"It's the rescue squad's. The ambulance," Arthur said.

He and the other black firefighters at the Dobbins station were listening to the sounds of the fire.

"You might be right. It's not no fire truck's."

A fire engine, whether it was a pumper, a tanker or a ladder truck, had a different sound than the police or rescue or EMT vehicles.

"No horns," someone said. "No claxon."

"They got those on the rescue. And the police," Arthur said. "But they don't sound like ours."

"Choppers coming in, too. Coming in and going out."

The eight actual members of the Dobbins' unit remained at the station but they had been joined by some of the women and older people in the community. They gathered in front like they would have for a fund-raising event, for a cookout and plate sale, where the men might have gathered early in the morning and started up the big fryer unit of their own and cooked, courtesy of a wholesale purchase from Capital, a thousand pounds of chicken fingers, sold to the public for $5.00 along with slaw, two slices of white bread and baked beans.

"You can't get near it," someone said to Arthur.

"I know that."

"No need to go where you're not wanted."

They were so close they could hear the bull horns, the speaker phone radio transmissions that they were monitoring already on their own channels, and they could see the smoke above the building. Watching it located the structure geographically in a way they debated, killing time and trying to discover something they could say to reduce the insult of being denied the opportunity to help.

"I thought that building was more to the left," one said.

"No. Right over those trees. Just aim your eye a thousand feet from the spire on that old station."

"I see that, but it don't look right. Maybe something else burning."

"Nothing else there. Now that's not there."

"We been lynched. They done lynched us again."

"Don't get that kind of talk started," Arthur said.

"Hung up like fools. Can't even go in the back door."

"Amen," another man said.

"Nothing's changed," someone said. "Nothing at all."

The group waited and watched. They looked back and forth from the fire site a few miles away, watching the different-colored smoke spread under the haze, watched it rise up and then break apart and go sideways, the way smoke in a room did when it hit a ceiling. They looked at that and then when there was something clear and understandable on the emergency radio frequency, they looked at the radio, as if it was a television, or had a screen and they could see something.

Behind them two technically advanced fire trucks idled, paid for by taxes and grants, maintained and staffed by volunteers who waited each day to be asked to do something good in the world, something heroic. Everyday all these men, all these people now gathered in front of the station went to work and did what they were asked to do, just like the people at Capital. There was nothing special about what they might have usually been doing at this time on a Tuesday morning, nothing special except they were all ready to be more than that, all ready to participate in the simple language of belief, of courage. They already were a part of the simple language of work each day, the talk and activity that produced a piece of fried chicken or a sock or a gasket or pack of staples that later someone, somewhere might use to force a group of papers to stay together, so that someone else, somewhere might read them and understand what to do that day.

But they were special at the same time, and they all waited for a chance to show it. They wanted to be more than usual, wanted to be good in a way that was spiritual, in a way that was close to Godliness, wanted the chance to prove what was inside, to act on the challenge of heroic endeavor, to be more than a person who packs a chicken breast or makes a pair of nylon stockings and was, in the usual day, full of bitterness and frustration and confusion and weighted under years of bad judgment, bad decisions, sunk by poor health, by debt, by impulse, by weakness, by human desire and need. The day, the hour, the moment had come when they could have been asked to be as good and strong and selfless and powerful as men and women could be, and they had been denied that chance.

CHAPTER 27

11:30 A.M.

There were doctors and nurses everywhere. The came to the site and they examined everyone. They knelt beside them on the grass, on the sidewalk, in the parking lots, in the street. They looked closely at each person, peering into eyes, down throats, and asking so many difficult questions.

"Are you pregnant?"

The woman seemed about the age of Ellie's mother, but Ellie was not registering in enough detail to be sure.

"I'm an obstetrician," she said. "We ask every woman this. Do you know?"

"I am," Ellie said. "I am pregnant."

They were in a room at the hospital. Everyone who'd been in the fire was in a hospital somewhere, in Charlotte or Raleigh or for those not so badly off, in Hamlet. No one was going home until the medical people were sure they were out of danger.

"How far along?"

"Maybe two months."

The doctor's voice was distant and though Ellie heard the

words, she felt like she was listening to a conversation between two other people in another room.

This is serious, the doctor said. This is very serious. You'll be okay, but your child may not. You've been in a state of what we call anoxia. You were close to asphyxiation but you were never unconscious.

"I wasn't?" Ellie asked. "It seemed like I was."

You were close, the doctor said. From what I can see and measure, you were close. And listen to me, Ellie, you don't have to look at me, I know your eyes hurt, but listen to me. Close your eyes and listen.

"Okay."

We won't be able to tell, the doctor said, if the fetus is viable after this kind of toxic exposure. Lots of young women abort early, from all kinds of trauma, and so a spontaneous abortion is possible.

"Oh gosh," Ellie said.

There is an increased chance, the doctor said, of ruptured membranes in the uterus. Young women who don't take care of themselves sometimes abort around 20 to 22 weeks. We see this, and we used to see this even more often. You may have that happen. We'll be looking after you carefully. You hear me? I will be here for you whenever you need me. But here's something else I have to tell you. And this will be almost worse. Are you up to hearing it now?

"Yes. I want to know."

There is a high probability that your baby, if you don't spontaneously abort, will be born with abnormalities. It could have brain damage, or cerebral palsey-esque afflictions, like blindness. I'm sorry. I'm so very sorry, Ellie. You have so much to think about now, and the next few months won't be easy. Do you have any questions?

"Oh God, I don't know. I just don't know what to say."

Everyone is here to help you, the doctor said. All of us. This whole town is here for you. Please know that. You might want to make a decision soon. If you decide that way, it'll be easier and safer than later. You understand that? Otherwise, no one is going to push you one way or the other. It's your decision. But think about it carefully. And long. And not just tonight or tomorrow, but over the next week or so. Think about what you will do the rest of your life. But this is your child, and no one will take it or interfere. Just remember what I said about the chances of trouble. And let me say something as a woman. Speaking to you as a woman. We have this great reserve of love and nurture and we want to offer it and use it. Sometimes it's the kind of thing that makes our lives very difficult. Sometimes we do that to ourselves. But either way, I'm here for you. We all are.

CHAPTER 28

Report Of Investigation by Medical Examiner: North Carolina Department of Environment, Health, and Natural Resources: Division of Postmortem Medicolegal Examination.

Jay Ammons:

Analyte: Carbon Monoxide: Greater than 70% in blood.

72 1/2 inches in height. 203 lbs.

Black hair with beard and mustache.

Eyes Brown.

Body temperature cold.

Teeth natural upper and lower.

Circumcised. Healed scar on belly left. Hand broken. Soot in nose and mouth.

Clothing: rubber boots, black tee shirt, white socks, blue jeans; white briefs.

Valuables: pocket knife; wallet; photos of children; misc. papers; 1-$5.00 bill. 72 cents in change; plastic toy from Wendy's Kid's Meal; car and other keys.

Lizzy Ammons:
   Analyte: Carbon Monoxide: Greater than 70% in blood.
   61 inches in height. 103 lbs.
   Brown hair, braided.
   Eyes brown.
   Body temperature cold.
   Teeth natural upper and lower.
   Clothing: leather tied shoes; argyle/white/gray socks; black
Levi's pants; apron; white panties; white bra; tee shirt with word
Mommy on front.
   Valuables: $2.12 in change; wedding ring; graduation type ring
"Raiders"; nail clippers; Lance Peanut Bar—crushed; photos of
children; keys.

Cecelia Locklear:
   Analyte: Carbon Monoxide greater than 30%.
   67 inches in height. 124 lbs.
   Hair blonde.
   Eyes gray/blue.
   Body temperature cold.
   Teeth natural upper and lower; face covered with soot; gravel
in mouth, nose, hair and ears; blisters on both hands, knees, face
and left back shoulder; grasping piece of white ceramic tile with
particle board in hand; small tattoo of woman on motorcycle at
waistline on belly; broken fingers on left hand; eyebrows, eyelashes missing; scar on neck, healed.
   Clothing: blue jeans; apron; pink panties; pink bra; yellow
shirt; red athletic shoes; red socks.
   Valuables: gold colored bracelet; silver ring with stone; red hair
clips; bottle of Tylenol; three pills in plastic bag of unknown ori-

gin; 83 cents in change; 3-$1 bills; 9-$20 bills; 1-$50 bill; gold chain necklace with pendant; piece of Kleenex; car keys.

Jessie Oxendine:
Analyte: Carbon Monoxide greater than 70%
64 inches in height; 106 lbs.
Hair black.
Eyes brown.
Body temperature cold.
Teeth mostly missing; eleven counted. Scars(healed) on arms, wrist, left cheek on face, across left breast, abdominal area (possibly C-section), palm of right hand, upper lip extending toward nose and up side of nostril; needle tracks in lower left arm; soot and gravel in mouth, nose, ears; dark red nail polish; shoulder dislocated.

Clothing: flowered skirt; wig; knee-high nylons; boots; blue smock; blue shirt, black lace bra, snap broken, straps tied together in knot; no panties.

Valuables: cigarette rolling papers; man's class ring in skirt pocket—Chargers; earrings, gold colored, pierced in ear; 73 cents in change; misc. papers; 1 child custody hearing summons; 1 lipstick; two Tampons; knife; 1 chicken breast wrapped in plastic, partially eaten, in skirt pocket; 1 antique wristwatch, Elgin Princess; photo of child.

Tony Silverman:
Analyte: Carbon Monoxide less than 60%
70½ inches in height; 145 lbs.
Hair brown / gray beneath.
Eyes brown—left clouded.

Body temperature cold.

Rigor 3+.

Teeth upper natural and appliance; lower natural; pink lips; soot in nose, mouth, left nostril packed solid; defib marks on chest; trach 1 ? inch; small tattoo upper arm, heart with letter L; small tattoo, lower belly, 'Rob', with heart design underneath; tattoo chest area, U.S. Marines with logo; uncircumcised; gravel and grit in skin of face, neck; pubic hair shaved.

Clothing: tight stretch pants; sleeveless tee shirt, words—Las Vegas 1990; low cut briefs; black leather armed forces style boots; black socks; red cowboy-style bandana around neck.

Valuables: wallet with papers; 1-$10 bill; 3-$1 bills; 67 cents in change; ring of keys on retractable cord; belt with Mack Truck buckle; gold ring with small diamond stone.

Rudolph Baker

Analyte: Carbon Monoxide less than 30%

65 inches in height; 169 lbs.

Hair gray.

Eyes Brown.

Body intact; temperature cold; Rigor 2+; Liver cherry red.

Teeth upper and lower appliance; right arm broken at elbow; knee broken; soot, grit and gravel in mouth and nose, in and around eyes.

Clothing: "Lance" uniform, shirt and pants with name, Rudy; boxer shorts; white undershirt; white socks; black leatherette shoes, steel-toed.

Valuables: large black wallet on chain; 3-$100 bills; 6-$20 bills; 3-$5 bills; 8-$1 bills; six quarters in pocket; misc. papers; keys; large analog watch, crystal broken; pocket knife with screw drivers;

large hexagonal key with "Lance" stamped on it, in leather sheath; silver crucifix on chain around neck; wedding band; high school ring—Mustangs.

Byrum O'Neal:
Analyte: Carbon Monoxide less than 50%
68½ inches in height; 164 lbs.
Hair Light Brown to Blonde.
Eyes Green/brown.
Body temperature cold; Rigor 1+
Teeth upper and lower natural; scars(healed): across skull from ear over the top to ear, poorly knitted at time of suture, sunken along line; grit, soot, and unidentified flakes in mouth, nostrils; under fingernails flakes of paint, splinters of wood, rubber or vinyl like substance.

Clothing: blue cotton slacks; tan shirt; boots; apron; torn hair net; white briefs; white undershirt, new, with price tag; white socks.

Valuables: watch; 1 key; wallet; laminated ID; three uncashed checks; 4-$10 bills; 1-$50 bill hidden; 6-$1 bills; 1-$5 bill; 8 quarters; misc. papers; set of tiny clothes from a Barbie and Ken doll, with small man's suit, cap, plastic loafers, sun bonnet and miniature radio and beach wear, folded inside a miniature suitcase; 1 audio tape case, no tape; three pieces of butterscotch candy; 1 Chapstick; small, convertible Matchbox style toy car; 1 folded piece of paper, written name 'Ellie' and phone number.

Summary:
Total dead: 25
Total injured and transported to hospitals: 49

Within three days the refrigerated bodies were back from the medical examiner's office. The local funeral homes were ready. They had ordered more of everything. The entire country had heard about the events, and groups of people from all over, representing helpful and unexpected agendas, showed up in Hamlet, set up shop, preached, performed, aided and reported. All the motel rooms within twenty miles were taken, and a writer from the *Charlotte Observer* stayed in the same one Ellie's dad had used and reported it had a door so warped it wouldn't latch and she had to shove her furniture against it at night and take her belongings with her during the day.

"Can I have fries?" Silas, Jay and Lizzy's son asked. Destiny was home with relatives.

There was a street theater production going on beside Hardees where the man and the boy pulled in to the lot. They had set up in the parking spaces of an empty store building.

"You can have anything you want," his grandfather said. "Anything on this earth."

The actors in the play beside Hardees were dressed in costumes. One man wore a half-human, half-pig head. One person was a chicken. The others were dressed in bib overalls and shower caps and aprons and boots.

"Just fries. And ketchup," Silas said. "Large fries."

The group was from MIMA, the Maoist International Movement of America. Their brochures, which were on a table, said: "We comprise the collection of existing or emerging Maoist internationalist parties for the English-speaking Capitalist revolutionary opportunity for the people."

"That's fine," his grandfather said. "Large fries is fine." He glanced at the group next door. Nothing in the name or in what they were doing was recognizable in any way. It looked like a bunch setting up a yard sale. He held his grandson's hand and went inside the restaurant.

The play began. The narrator spoke.

"The greedy pig owners of Capitalist Foods had a captive work force," he said. The people dressed in shower caps and bib overalls leaned over like they were picking cotton and moved as if their backs hurt and they dragged slowly around the parking lot, walking toward some central point.

"They were held down by low wages."

They bent further toward the ground.

"They were the victims of the never-ending plantation mentality of endless work and low pay. They were trapped in the Black Belt of low-wage labor."

Cars drove by. The human dressed as the chicken was put on a table and the worker actors pulled at the feathers. The pig man actor stood behind the people in the shower caps and cracked a whip in the air, over their backs.

Inside Hardees, Edward saw Lois and Carly. Their eyes were still red and swollen and the skin on the very outer edge of their nostrils was abraded.

"I'm so proud to see you out," Edward said to Lois and hugged her to him. He held her for a long time, patted her back, pulled her head against his shoulder, clasped it firmly and then leaned across the booth and kissed Carly on the cheek. "Are you okay now?" he asked the girl.

"I think so."

"I'm so sorry about your loss," he said.

"Hello, angel," Lois said to Silas. She put her hand on top of his head. "Are you hungry?"

Outside at the production, a woman read from a paper while the other actors, still in costume, stood behind her.

"Be aware that chickens are oppressed by the same things that have been oppressing workers throughout history, that have oppressed women, that same mentality, that same predatory, masculine greed."

"What's that over there?" Edward asked, looking at the window from her booth where he had joined her. "I don't understand. Do you?"

"Maybe," she said, and looked back at the signs and read them and watched the drama a moment. "Yes, I think I do."

The fries had not been ready when he'd ordered them for Silas. A worker in a cap and apron brought them to the table.

"Is this for this perfect little boy here?" she asked, clearly oversolicitous. Everyone in town was concerned, hurt and stunned by the loss.

Silas nodded. He took a single fry and swirled it in his ketchup, making patterns. Carly, wearing a scarf on her head, stared into her hamburger like a fortune teller, hypnotized, lost somewhere in thought.

CHAPTER 30

Reverend Bishers spoke at Antonio's funeral at the A. M. E. Church ceremony. He was above the congregation, behind the pulpit, dressed in exquisite black ecclesiastical raiment. He was a man in good with his people and with God. He was imposing and sturdy and understood the world of work and life and the spirit. He had earned his living in construction trades for years while putting himself through school. He knew the connection and the distance between good works, and work.

Outside the church, a freshly washed, perfectly waxed lime-sherbet green Cadillac was parked. It belonged to Lois and Carly now. No will, no probate attorney or judge had assigned it. It was simply that it would be. The right thing would be done. It was all of value that Antonio had had. Uncle Arthur had made sure she got it. He had cleaned it. He had arranged to pay Antonio's family $6,000 for it, but had not told anyone that he did. Inside the church, at the front, with the lid open, lay Antonio. He looked content, handsome and dignified as in life, modest and at peace.

He did not appear, to Carly, to have suffered or been hurt.

Reverend Bishers began with comfort and blessings and the

welcoming of visitors and those from out of town, by which he meant the reporters who stood against the wall behind the last pews, looking awkward, distinctly out of place, sleepy but respectful. He then moved toward his metaphors, which he'd spent the night before composing:

"So I'm recalling Joshua. And I'm wondering if the walls will have to come down now. They will be knocked apart into their origins, into their pieces, one concrete block, one brick, one four-inch-by-four-inch section of tile, one door jamb, one long run of 14-gauge, three-wire Romex cable that failed to illuminate. When things got bad, it failed to provide light. Only one thing, only one thing ever known to mankind never fails to illuminate.

"What man had constructed and wired into that building had carried, until the last moment, the electricity back and forth. It was what we call alternating current, not direct. We know and have direct current, direct connection, but this, like what man has made, is alternating. It makes a circuit, like I do, and like my own circuit, and like yours, if that path is broken, if that journey the electrical current takes is broken in any one place, and the electricity in the wire cannot return home, it fails. It stops right where it is broken. As many of you know I wired some of your houses and amen, they are standing and the journey is complete, there is no break, and the lights shine. Amen.

"The power that is generated leaves its source and moves along the wires in an endless circle, and endless cycle, from the source, through the house, through God's house or a house where chickens were processed, it's all the same to the source, to the power, to CP&L, or to God, it's the same. The power is sent. The lights are lit. Illumination. We are given illumination.

"But it failed. A few days ago, it failed. Somebody will tear out all those wires, all the paths of earthly electric illumination and they will strip the cable of the insulation, and sell the copper for scrap. For the weight of the copper that remained. There is no scrap in human life. None at all. Born blessed and holy, we die the same. God does not discriminate, chicken plant or sanctuary of God, it's the same to him. No scrap. All holy. All pure. All blessed. The lights went out. The air was bad. The exits were locked. The only way out for some was up, and that way is never blocked."

Carly stared at her father, ten feet away in front of her. Uncle Arthur was on one side of her and her mother on the other. Her father's stillness spoke to her more than the words from the pulpit. She was afraid differently from when she'd been in the freezer, breathing inside the cardboard box, and surviving. She had understood she would survive. But now, death was what she saw in front of her. She understood though not in any way she could have told it, the stillness, how the soul evaporated and moved on, the face there and not there, not the same, like a drawing of her father, like a blind person who could not see her, that was how she felt, that he did not know she was there, and she would have to find a way to let him know she remembered everything. She understood that he was gone and that it was the stillness that nothing living could ever imitate, that was death.

CHAPTER 31

If not for a car wreck where Cecelia had totaled her Caprice, if not then for increased insurance payments, if not for running away that night from a bad scene at home, if not for thinking too hard about why she was in her car and not with her family, if not for seeing her life in front of her and not the curve and tree, if not for tires slick because there was no money for better ones after paying to eat and rent and clothe, if not for bad luck, if not for car payments to get to work to earn enough only to make the payments on the car used to get to work and keep it repaired which took the money that might have gone to pay for health insurance, if not for taxes she could not escape that fell on her and her family with no way out, if not for politicians who owed her nothing, if not for impoverishment so blinding that she couldn't even see a hickory tree in front of her, couldn't even see a way out of her life, couldn't see even a week into her future, only the day and then the next, but not until then, if not for all of that, she would not have been working there and would be alive.

If not for Jay having the decency to show up at work even though he knew he should be applying elsewhere, if not for understanding that if he didn't show up, the work would not be done that was needed to fix the fryer to keep the other people working who would then be sent home with nothing to do, if not for the effort to play along and listen to his supervisor and his bad advice, if not for his effort to rise above his inexperience and repair the part, if not for his genteel nature and sense of duty, if not for inheriting that from his father, if not for falling in love with Lizzy, if not for their understanding the rare nature of their compatibility, if not for signing finance papers and debt and the understanding that once you agree to something, you have to do it, if not for meeting after work at the car and discussing what they'd seen heard and done each day on the way home, if not for *not* understanding that he and she were in danger, if not for trusting that things would always be better, if not for believing and trusting, he and she would still be alive.

It was the same for everybody there. If not for one particular bad day, one particular bad decision, if not for endless debt, if not for the fatigue of impoverishment, if not for the careless arrogance, and the bravado and bluff of incompetence, if not for the adventure of desire, if not for the cunning and mistaken simplicity of that desire, if not for the stealthy confusion of just exactly what happened and how to get out of what happened that took over a person's life like a virus, like a single Anthrax spore inhaled one day that then took host and grew, if not for pure bad luck, if not for there but for the grace of God go all of us, none of them would have been there, working there, and none of them would have died.

CHAPTER 32

A group of men working in the back room of Central Carolina Hydraulics stopped talking when the woman they had named Gitumee Bunoon came through the battered, double swinging doors. The doors had strike plates and kick plates, but they were beat up anyway from handcarts and forklifts bumping through them all day long.

"Looks like we lost one of our customers," she said.

The doors swung closed behind her and then rebounded and swung a few times again, each time shutting a bit more until they were even. The way the room got quiet when she entered and the doors slapped in and out as she walked toward the men made her entrance look like the old west, and a woman, of all things, had entered a saloon.

"Yes ma'am," one of the men said while she walked past them.

"That was a bad fire over there," someone said. "She's right. That place is toast."

"Yeah, burnt toast."

"You just can't ever tell what'll happen when you get up in the morning."

Two men walked away from the group and went back to work at one of the long, greasy metal tables that they, themselves, had years earlier built out of quarter-inch steel plate and two-inch pipe legs. They had welded them together and raised the height of the table top from what had been factory supplied so they didn't have to bend over while they worked.

"That was some bad luck over at that place," Puddin said.

"I know."

"A bad way to go."

"It sure is."

"Damn fried a whole bunch of them."

"It did."

"That was just some plain bad luck."

"I know."

"Smoked them."

"Yep."

"Smoke, smoke, smoke them cigarettes."

"You got it," the first one said and kept working on a new hose he was putting together.

"Locked the doors on them."

"That was bad."

"That's why they died," he said. "The television said they couldn't get out."

"I heard that."

"Shit happens."

"Yep."

"Give me land, lots of land but don't fence me in," Puddin said while gathering up a handful of fittings and laying them out in front of him.

"Yep."

"Where we going to lunch today. KFC again?"

"That'll be all right."

"A visit to the Colonel."

"You got it."

"Colonel Harlan M. Sanders, 'M' for millionaire," Puddin said, fiddling with the fittings, rolling them around in his palm like marbles or beads.

"Made some money, didn't he?"

"Reminds me of old John Bears Fortipton."

"Who?"

"Everybody kind of always thinks something like a million dollars out of the blue sky will happen to them."

"Yep."

They kept working. The first man measured out a length of hose and the second man fed him the fittings, one by one, as he needed them. After they finished an order, they tagged it and moved it to the side.

"Ken-tuck-eee Fried Chicken," Puddin said, dragging out the words and looking at his watch. "Original or Spicy. I reckon some of them folks can go to work over there," he added. "Cooking that. Chicken's chicken. They know how to do that."

"Yep."

"Twenty minutes," he said, making a tower out of the fittings, setting one on top of another like a child playing with blocks, going as high as he could until they fell. "Can't see it from my house," he mumbled, walking off toward a bin across the room. "No sir. No siree. No speekee Englis," he said louder.

"How's that?"

"That's what that Mexicali boy said to me the other day. No speekee."

The first man stopped work for a moment. His mouth felt dry. He picked up a can of Pepsi he'd opened earlier in the morning and took a sip and then set it back on the metal shelf among the debris.

"Old men, you know," Puddin said, returning with another handful of brass and copper, "they could hit a spittoon at twenty feet. I seed them do it many a time."

"Yep."

"Ready to go?"

"I guess."

"Let's go see the Colonel. They do chicken right."

CHAPTER 33

"I always thought I was brave. I've always thought that," Ellie said.

She and Ricky were in their meeting place where the light fixture hung by the wires. She stared at it after she said that, like she had so often, and spoke nothing more even though Ricky had the sense she was about to continue.

"I meant to fix that," he said. He had followed her eyes and realized where she was looking.

"I'm so sad now," she said. "I don't see how I'll ever be anything else."

"People get over things. I guess."

"Do they?"

"I don't know. Maybe they don't."

I asked my mother why she never told me that the Rayburn Funeral Home was our home, her home, my ancestral home. How could she not tell me that? She said it had never been hers. I asked her how it could be that she chose not to think about her own mother growing up there and she said her mother had only lived there a little while and then the family had to sell it, and they sold everything and it seemed, she said, just like everything else in her life that had been a disappointment and a loss, just another unstoppable event and nothing to do with her. I have to ask these things now because I want to understand how it is that I seem to be more like someone else and not her, but the woman in the diary pages.

"We have to go back now," Ellie said. "But I want to tell you something first."

The only reason I found out that it was my ancestral home is because Daddy is in there now, dead, and we have to go there and that's when everything started, this new life, and I found out about it, it's like no one knew or cared so no one ever told me. Now my own father is now laid out dead in a house that was somehow his own house, or could have been by marriage. If things had been different. If things had gone better.

I want to explore the house. I wonder if the upstairs rooms are used. I need to find Emily's room. Mom told me that there was another house that they'd all lived in, Anita as a child and Millicent, and it was still here, but no one talked about it, either, just a simple, two-story, nothing-special house on Pryor Street that I haven't yet gone by to see. So maybe that's the way it is, that's how you get past things. You forget that they were ever important.

"I'm going with you," he said. "I want to stay with you all day. If you'll let me."

"He was coming to get me," she said. "He was trying to find me. He was trying to save me," she said, but just barely got it out.

I guess if you can believe in something then it doesn't matter if you don't believe in yourself. If you don't yet believe in yourself. It's like I imagine I could believe in this child no matter what she or he is or has, and then I have this sick feeling because I'm afraid I can't. I imagine I can and it seems like I am doing it, like I am changing just by thinking it, but then this feeling like fear, but not like darkness and suffocation, not like that.

"I'm sorry," Ricky said. "I'm so sorry."

She reached her hand to his face, to pat him, to thank him for saying that and feeling it, and she saw her own hand moving slowly, disembodied. She felt his own wet cheeks. She leaned far back and looked at him. She wanted to see his face, what he looked like sad and softened, and changed. She wanted to be with him. For a long time.

I thought I was holding onto Byrum but it wasn't him and so he died because I let him go and then later I am thinking that I shouldn't let anything go anymore. That I can't do that anymore. That I need to hold on. I am thinking that all the time, what it means. I've read all the pages now, everything from Emily's diary.

"I need to tell you something before the day is over," she said. "Don't let me forget."

He does look different now. What happened to me happened to him. I still have the red abrasions around my nostrils and my eyes are still scary, like they've been in chlorine, like I've swum all day in a heavy chlorine pool. The smell wouldn't come out of my hair so I cut it even shorter. I cut so much of it off. When he saw me, when he came to get me that morning and saw me like this, he went into the bathroom and when he came out his was cut off just like mine. He made it just like I did, just a scissors hack job. I know when he holds me he must smell the death on me, but he hasn't said anything. He hasn't even flinched. I am looking for it, but he hasn't shown it.

"I was trying to remember something, also. I saw in the paper yesterday that Frank Capra died the day of the fire," he told her. "A kind of hero to us at one time."

"He died? Truly? That day?"

"Yes."

It's not death that smells. That's not it. I've thought about what it must be. It's the struggling life that was left behind that was all around me, the burned dreams like scraps of paper, that's all they were in the end, dreams of a better life that just burned like single sheets of paper, that flimsy and insubstantial. It was the effort to live that burned out of the bodies that I smelled, that sad force of effort that went nowhere, the smell and sound of smoky voices.

You know how people say she had a smoky voice, well, now I know what that is, really is, the songs that are sung as people die. If I had turned on Byrum's tape recorder then I would have them, but I would never want anyone to hear them. I'd have recorded the sounds that no one should ever hear because you wouldn't want to know what it sounds like to die like that. I did record them, though. I have them in my head. When they start I have a vertigo, like I'm falling in a tunnel of those sounds and they are the walls of the tunnel, the swirling walls that I am spinning inside of. Those sounds. Those sounds are why I will never be the same again. That and the smells.

"When are the funerals?" Ricky asked.

"Daddy's is this afternoon. At two. Then, a little later, Byrum's. Gwen's coming by to go to both of them with us. I need to go home."

"I'll follow you. Then we can ride together to the funerals."

I play the tape. I listen to Byrum's voice. I play it and make myself cry. I do it again and again. I think of him and of Emily and I hear them. I play it and I listen and I cry. I hear the words. I think of my own child. I think again how I must hold on to the people in my life. All of them who love me and who I love and who I am to love, no matter what.

"We need to leave now," she said. "Mom needs me and I need to be there with her."

I am the life that must be lived. I am the girl that was. I am him and me. I am the child and the mother and the daughter. I am all of them.

The End

Afterword

The working life for these people began as a floor. That was all it was for a time, before the walls went up, the roof went on. They stood on it. They moved back and forth while they made the sweetest of confections out of butter and cream and pecans and cocoa. That floor was put there on that piece of land by men who dug the footings, chopped through the roots, dislodged the rocks, squared up and made sheer the side walls of the excavation. The men mixed and poured the slab and had work to do when there was little to be had. They arrived each morning and created this floor. It contained, from then on, people who had faith, who believed.

They were the ice cream makers and the form fillers making up the special orders of fancy chocolate-dipped Christmas trees and Santa Clauses with red and green food coloring dots laid in by hand on the warm chocolate, some of which dropped right onto the old slab, the same place that later the chicken fat and mangled body parts and hot, spitting grease dropped.

The base of it all remained though, the foundation and the smooth concrete. It remained like a dance floor where the music

would be the language of work, a floor like a stage, full of ama-
teurs trying to figure out how to say what they had to say, how
to move, how to enter and leave and how to speak what they
couldn't easily find words to say. Because they didn't know how
to understand their parts in that drama, they worked. They simply worked. They showed up and did their job.

After the walls were gone, after the roof was gone, after the
machines had stopped rattling and squealing and were removed,
then the floor remained, cleaned off and now a monument,
slightly raised above the earth.

It became a memorial for the work that had been done upon
it, itself all that was needed to remember the people who had
labored day in and out on it, a monument on its back rather than
upright. It was spread out the way that people themselves had
worked, side by side, a space that occupied the amount of earth
that would have held the same number of people working nearby one another, the solace, the fear, the loyalty, the confusion and
the bitterness, all of that had room to remain between where the
people would have been, room for all of that and all of them.

It was not a spire which signified only the ideal of man and
heaven and hope, but the actual stage where the drama of daily
life and work was put on with relentless regularity, the same
drama each day. The people showed up, were told where to stand,
how to move, and what was expected. They showed up with some
faith that something decent and hopeful would happen, that their
work would be rewarded, their lines said in such a way that they
would prevail and would be allowed to work another day, which
is all they could think to ask at the time—what do I do, how do
I do it and will I be paid. They never asked if they would die. They
never considered it. It wasn't supposed to happen.

The slab remained, then, after the building was torn down. The lot was cleared and the scorched and smoked vegetation removed. The slab became the gravestone, a wide marker on which for 70 years people had talked among themselves all day long, creating the belief and the hope that there was a reason they were doing what they were asked, creating by what they said an understanding among themselves—that because they spoke the same language and endured the same hardship, they would prevail.

AND THEN THIS HAPPENED

In January of 1992, the State of North Carolina fined Capital Foods $808,150 for violations that included locked doors and no emergency lighting.

In March of 1992, Ellie gave birth three weeks premature to a healthy baby girl. She and Richard were married and she moved to Chapel Hill to be with him while he finished school.

In September of 1992, Charlie was sentenced to 19 years, 11 months in jail. There was a plea bargain that allowed George Bonny Russell to get off with no time.

In 1994, Mojo Nixon wrote a song called *Hamlet Chicken Plant Disaster*. It was on Jello Biafra's label, Alternative Tentacle Records. ". . . down in hamlet they had a chicken plant sure did explode them tar heels trapped like burnin rats cuz the boss man chained the door closed, my mama was born in a town called hamlet, sleepy little place on the seaboard line, my papa worked on the railroad and my granny went out of her mind . . . "

In February, 1995, Charlie was denied parole.

In April, 1997, Charlie was released from jail early. He was told he would not be allowed to return to North Carolina except for medical care.

In 1998, a writer from the *Charlotte Observer* reported that George was wearing wire rim glasses, had a goatee and worked in a restaurant near Atlanta. The writer said George gave whatever spare money he had to his father, who was doing menial labor but would not say where or what kind of work it was.

In 2001, on the ten-year anniversary of the fire, a writer for the *News and Observer* interviewed a former worker, who said she had gotten about $200,000 in a settlement from injuries from the fire, but that most of it was gone, and that her husband, who used to work as a chicken catcher in the live haul part of the business, had left her, and that she had headaches so bad she wanted to split her own head open with an ax to try to make them stop, that she took injections straight into her own skull to relieve the pain, and that she didn't have any work, couldn't find any and wouldn't be able to work if she had.

In the Spring of 2002, Ellie graduated from N.C. State with a degree in textile design. She and Richard, who became a lawyer, live in Greensboro, where he practices law and she works for Burlington Industries. Louise visits Caroline, her granddaughter, often.

ACKNOWLEDGEMENTS AND SOURCES

Articles from *The Charlotte Observer, The News and Observer, The Richmond County Times, The NY Times, The Washington Post, Time Magazine.*

NCOSH—North Carolina Occupational Safety and Health Project

RAFI—Rural Advancement Foundation International

Richard J. Barnes and Dick Barnes Jr., of MelloButtercup Ice Cream Co. Inc.

Dr. Dean McPhail

Dr. Joseph Horrigan

Dr. Lisa Amaya-Jackson, Duke University.

Dissertation by Ruth R. DeRosa; Duke University, Dept. of Psychology

More Than a Memory; A publication of the Hamlet Centennial Committee, which, in turn, got its sources from "newspapers, receipts, scrapbooks, letters and . . . anyone who might have knowledge of the early years of Hamlet."

The War on the Ground; by Colin John Bruce

The Destruction of Dresden; by David Irving

ARC Insight—sections inspired by an article entitled—*A Self Made Man.*

The Tragedy at Imperial Food Products; Committee on Education and Labor; House of Representatives; 102 Congress.

N.C. OSHA Compliance Special Report on Capital Food Products.

Office of the Chief Medical Examiner; NC Dept. of Environment, Health and Natural Resources.

FEMA; United States Fire Administration; Chicken Processing Plant Fires—Hamlet, North Carolina and North Little Rock, Arkansas

Reference Guide for Solving Poultry Processing Problems. Julie Northcutt. University of Georgia, Cooperative Extension Service.

OSHA Ergonomic Report in Dressing and Cutting of Chickens.

And with thanks to: Ellen Levine; Carolyn Sakowski and everyone at Blair; Anne, Joyce, Peggy, and Melissa at Kachergis Book Design; Susan, Haven, Dannye, Christa, Keebe, and Nancy.